NINE MEN'S MORRIS

BY

JOY PEACH

Authors
On Line

Visit us online at www.authorsonline.co.uk

An Authors OnLine Book

ISBN 0 7552 0190 6

Authors OnLine Ltd
40 Castle Street
Hertford SG14 1HR
England

This book is also available in e-book format, details of which are available at www.authorsonline.co.uk

This book is dedicated to Dianna and Stanley Doubtfire who took me to France with them many years ago. And to Michael Legat who generously helped me knock it into shape.

But above all, it is for my splendid parents who, in spite of the difficulties of the years during and after the Second World War, brought up the seven of us – in no way do they resemble the disastrous parents in the story.

By the same author:

SOLITAIRE, published by Prospero Books 1996
and available through Authors OnLine

Chapter One

"Attention, s'il vous plaît, Mesdames, Messieurs - will you please adjust your watches. It is now seven-fifty-four exactly - vingt heures moins six . . ."

Rosemary wound on the delicate Victorian one Edward had given her. "It was my grandmother's . . ."

"Oh, Edward - it's gorgeous ! Gorgeous !"

"Well, it is a rather special occasion, isn't it, eh !"

A year since they first met and her Big Five-O.

" . . . and will passengers with cars now descend to their vehicles and prepare to disembark. Merci !"

Rosemary was in no hurry to join the stampede to the car deck. She stood a little longer leaning on the rail. The pilot directing operations from the back . . .

"The *stern*, love," Edward would have corrected her.

. . . from the stern was having trouble swinging the ferry round against the wind. It had been a rough crossing.

"Alors, doucement !" he called urgently into his walkie-talkie. "Gently does it !"

Betsy was right, she thought, finding herself suddenly alone in the last piercing rays of sunshine, I should have cancelled the damn trip. And settling her sunglasses firmly into place to conceal her pain, Rosemary made her way below.

"Why don't you cancel it, Ma ?" Betsy had said. "You'll be miserable on your own. You know you will."

"You could come with me, love. It would be fun together."

"No chance. We'll be back at college by then. Term starts on the first."

"Perhaps I could switch the booking. For later on ? When do you break up for the summer ?"

"I've got a holiday job, don't forget. All summer." Betsy was going to Italy with an MP's family. As au pair, looking after his three small children. "And I'll have reading to do for college. Serious reading. Three months off doesn't mean three months holiday."

1

So that was it. Rosemary had come as arranged for the first two weeks in May. And she had come alone.

On the car deck in her faithful old Morris Minor (pale blue and much-loved), she was jammed in tight between a white 'Jag' and a camping van which seemed to have at least half-a-dozen children in the back among mountains of bedding and gumboots and saucepans. There were two piles of surf-boards strapped to the roof, and several bicycles clipped onto a special contraption at the back.

Everything but the double-drainer, thought Rosemary, as she followed the heavily laden camper down the ramp and onto French soil.

"We're going to France !" Rosemary had announced, coming home from an evening with Edward. "Phaw ! What a stink ! Whatever's cooking ?"

"Miranda's latest concoction - birch bark, or some such."

"It's supposed to produce the most beautiful shade of orange, birch bark," Miranda their hippy lodger had said. A homeless waif, she had turned up on their doorstep the Christmas before last, the new-born Tommy in a sling, and had somehow settled in. "Kind of bright caramel. The wool looks pretty good already, and it's got to simmer a while yet."

"As I was saying . . ." Rosemary had said pointedly.

"You're going to France, you and Edward. That sounds fun." And Betsy had put aside her Biology essay to fill the kettle.

"We're taking a *gîte* . . ."

"A *what* ?" Miranda had asked, hanging another batch of nappies on the old fashioned airer above the Aga.

"You know - a gîte. One of those French holiday cottages. We've got it all organised."

"Just the two of you ?"

"Just the two of us. Three weeks tomorrow."

Hooking her wild red hair behind her ears with her thumbs, Miranda had settled back to her spinning.

"Show us where, then, Ma," Betsy had said, rummaging in the corner cupboard until she found the atlas.

"Half way down on the left," Rosemary had told them, peeling off her baggy brown jersey, one of Miranda's early creations, and slinging it onto the big scrubbed table with her striped canvas shoulder bag. "An inch or two in from the Atlantic."

"Oh, Ma ! On the west coast, don't you mean ? You are an idiot !"

"No, not on the coast. *There*." And Rosemary had pin-pointed it for them, somewhere between Poitiers and Limoges. "That's about it. Edward will show us in the morning."

"It's a hell of a long way south, isn't it ? It'll be a full day's drive once you've landed."

"It won't be too bad. We can share the driving. We're taking my car. It's more reliable than his old bus."

"They drive on the wrong side of the road, don't they ?" Miranda had said. "Jolly confusing, I should think."

But Rosemary was managing fine.

WELCOME TO FRANCE said the overhead signs as she drove out of the dock gates. REMEMBER - DRIVE ON THE RIGHT.

There's nothing to it, she thought, following the stream of GB plates towards the motorway. I can't think why I was so anxious. And she swung off to join the traffic for the south.

"Once we're on the right road," Edward had said that far away evening as they pored excitedly over maps and brochures, "once we're on the road we'll stop somewhere for the night. Start the journey proper next morning. Fresh and early."

"About here, perhaps," she had suggested, following the red road down the Michelin map with her finger. "Lisieux."

"Yes," he had said. "That looks about right. Let's see if they recommend a nice little family hotel, shall we."

"Le Cheval Blanc, s'il vous plaît ?" Rosemary asked hesitantly now, drawing up in the tree-lined *Place*, and testing her rusty French on a group of teenagers sprawling around the fountain.

It wasn't far. Through the traffic lights and round the corner.

"Oui, oui, Madame," said Monsieur le Patron, carrying her overnight bag up two flights of marble stairs. "Numéro Onze."

Numéro Onze, Rosemary thought, flinging herself and her belongings across the big bouncy bed. It would be bloody Numéro Onze !

"Room Number Eleven, Sir," the receptionist had said, giving Edward a funny look. That night. The night they had decided to stay up in London. Their First Night.

They had gone up to see the Summer Exhibition at the Royal Academy.

"I can't believe it !" Rosemary had said, as they stood together in front of her Spring Meadow. "My painting in a proper exhibition. Wow !"

"It's one of the best things here," he'd said fiercely. "They'd have been crazy to reject it."

"Oh, Edward . . ." She had put out her hand shyly, timidly, and caught hold of his.

They had sat together on a bench, hand-in-hand, watching people enjoying her picture.

"Oh, I like that one."

"Damn good, yes"

"So full of sunshine . . ."

"Such dazzling daisies . . ."

"What's it called, dear ? You've got the catalogue."

"Just a minute. Here we are. *Spring Meadow* by Rosemary Richardson."

"Well, she's certainly got something. I really like that one . . ."

"And so do I," Edward had whispered, squeezing her hand till it hurt. "I like the picture, and I like the artist, and I think we should have a slap-up meal to celebrate. And then . . ."

"Yes . . . ?"

"Come on," he had said, pulling her to her feet. "Suddenly I'm ravenous."

They had had lunch in an Italian place in Soho.

"I used to come here in my student days," Edward had told her.

They took a river bus up the Thames. They bought one another small mementoes in Carnaby Street.

"Oh, Edward !" she had said clipping on the dangly ear-rings he had found for her. "Rainbows !"

And when she discovered a T-shirt to match, with a rainbow right across the front, he had stripped off alongside the stall and put the new one on there and then. In the street.

It had been a good day.

"A double room, please ?" he had asked the po-faced girl at the reception desk.

"Twin beds, Sir ?"

"Double," he had said as if affronted. "And with a private bathroom, of course."

"Room Number Eleven, Sir," she had said then, primly. "On the first floor. Williams will show you up."

4

"She thinks I'm your mother," Rosemary had said, hugging him to her once they were alone.

"Who cares what the silly old cow thinks. She's only jealous."

And afterwards, dopey with loving, "Mm ! I'd begun to think we'd never get round to it, Rosie Richardson, my love."

She had run her hands lightly along his spine, learning the geography of him with joy. The slenderness of his limbs. The life and strength in his firm young flesh. The marvel of the soft dark hair swirling down from his belly . . .

"Mm !" He'd sighed sleepily, nuzzling into her breast. Like Miranda's young Tommy. "What a good thing it was *my* gallery you came to, eh, with your landscapes ?"

I'm a fool, she thought now, in this big empty bed in Room Number Eleven in the Hotel Cheval Blanc in Lisieux. That's all behind me.

There was a mini-bar, she noticed, between the bidet and the dressing-table. Ah, good - whisky ! She tipped the miniature bottle into a glass with a shot of Perrier Water, and tossed it back like an old soak.

My first night on French soil, she thought with excitement such as she hadn't expected to feel again. And the moment her head discovered the best way to adapt to the hard heavy bolster, Rosemary was asleep.

* * *

Chapter Two

The market noises woke her at dawn.

Downstairs, the plump patron got up from his own breakfast to whip the crumby paper cloth from the table by the open window, and spread a clean one for her on top of the red and white gingham.

"Bonjour, Madame."

He brought her a black enamelled coffee pot, a blue and white jug of steaming milk. Sipping the fragrant brew from the deep lugged bowl with dancing peasants painted round it, Rosemary felt well and truly abroad.

Most people, judging from the adverts on the telly, the Travel Supplements in the Sunday papers, most people seemed to manage a holiday in the sun every year. Maybe more than one.

She had only ever been abroad once before. Years ago. With the school trip to Paris. In the Fourth Form. A life time ago.

"Madame has slept well ?"

The croissants arrived, wrapped in a linen napkin, hot and crusty. There were delicate curls of pale butter floating in a small glass dish of water. A pot of apricot jam.

When she paid the bill, she checked the map on the wall behind the reception desk.

"I can help you, Madame ?"

"I'm making for Poitiers, Angoulême . . ."

"Eh, bien - follow the traffic to the second roundabout. It's well sign-posted from there."

She took her bag out to the car, and wedged it back in place among the luggage on the back seat. A little fruit would be nice on the long drive south. She slipped over into the busy square where the market was in full swing although it was barely seven o'clock.

What bustle! What colour! There were stalls of fruit, flowers, fish. Cheeses - white wheels of Brie, blue cheese, goats milk cheese, Petit Suisse in paper sleeves, Camembert. The vegetable stalls were bright with aubergines, peppers, huge tomatoes, frilly lettuce, artichokes. A long trestle table was entirely covered with quail, no bigger than budgies, plucked and trussed for the pot. Several stalls sold nothing but oysters. Others several different varieties of mushroom : brown, orange, black, cream and white.

An old woman squatted on a low stool on the cobbles, her produce spread out around her : parsley in a big blue bowl, a basket of brown eggs, half-a-dozen pats of home churned butter laid out on cabbage leaves, a few strings of garlic, pears stored carefully through the winter, and a bucket of daisies. At her feet two white ducks sat in a cardboard box cheerfully awaiting their fate.

With a baguette under her arm, a wedge of Brie, two golden pears, and a scoop of wild strawberries cushioned in damp moss, Rosemary went back to the car.

In no time, she was clear of the town, and weaving her way south through the farmsteads and orchards of Normandy.

It's a bit like Somerset, she thought. The timber-framed barns and cottages, lop-sided and weather-worn, dotted down among gnarled fruit trees foaming with blossom still, pink and white.

A lot like Somerset . . .

Suddenly, with a stab of pain, Rosemary was back in Isle St Agnes. Back in Aunt Mary's cottage. Was it only four days since the funeral ? Four days since they had carried the fierce old lady across Atyeo's Orchard through the long damp grass to the churchyard, the buttercups splashing their freshly pressed mourning with bright dabs of gold.

"Walk ! You've got to be joking. What if it rains ?" Frances, the eldest of Rosemary's three older sisters, had said over the phone. Learning with horror the night before the funeral the plans that had been made. "But we must have cars, Rosie. And a hearse. Must do it properly. What will people think ?"

"Never mind that. It's what she wanted. We planned it all years back. Soon after poor Mother went. This is exactly what Aunt Mary wanted. OK ?"

"When my turn comes," Aunt Mary had announced as she and Rosemary sorted through Mother's bits and pieces, her drawers and desk and cupboards, the evening after *that* funeral, "when it comes to my turn, I want none of this nonsense. No pomp and no damn ceremony. Remember now, Rosie. I'm relying on you, my lovely."

Heavens ! At Mother's funeral I was expecting Betsy, Rosemary thought. And look at her now, a grown woman herself, just about. Poor Mother.

"God willing, he'll take me while the blossom's out," Aunt

Mary had said, bringing the subject up again six weeks later, the day she'd driven across Wiltshire to see the new baby, five day old Betsy. "But whatever the season, I want no limousines, no mourning. It's no more than a step through the orchard to the Churchyard. Those strapping young fellows of Arthur Lock's can easily manage that short haul."

"Oh, Aunt Mary . . ."

"My, that would be a splendid thing. To be carried shoulder high between the trees, with buttercups under foot, and the bees busy in the apple blossom."

"Please, don't talk that way. Not today. With Mother scarcely cold herself. And you've not said a word to the baby."

"You're right, Rosie. And I'll say no more except this. That's the way I want it when the time comes. And you're the one to see to it for me. You let me down, and I'll come back to haunt you, I swear I will. Now then, let me make us a nice pot of tea, my lovely. Then I'll have a cuddle of this little lamb of yours."

And later, with the baby safely in her cradle, and five year old Billy sitting quietly at the table with his colouring book, Aunt Mary had said, "I'm glad you're naming her after your Mother, my girl. That would have pleased her no end, poor soul. A good old family name, right enough, Betsy. Your own Grandmother was a Betsy too."

"You done her proud, my gal !" Old Charlie, one of Aunt Mary's most ardent admirers had confided to Rosemary, leaning heavily on her shoulder as they followed the sprightlier mourners across Atyeo's Orchard last Tuesday morning, his First World War wound troubling him in his grief. "Mary always was such a one for the April Blow. My - how she would have enjoyed this send-off."

The family were not so easy to please.

"Damned lucky it isn't raining," Henry had sniffed to his tight-lipped wife. As the oldest, the head of the family now, he and Dolly walked immediately behind the coffin. "Could have been a fiasco."

But it hadn't rained. The coffin was smothered in petals that flurried round them in the sharp breeze, brightening the drab hats and coats and suits like confetti.

"Couldn't have asked for a better day," Old Charlie said, for all to hear, pausing to catch his breath against a gnarled Bramley.

8

"A mercy she didn't linger," a neighbour was saying behind them.

"'Tis a cruel thing, a stroke."

"Aye, 'tis a cruel thing to be rendered speechless."

"And for Mary Petherton of all people, speechless and paralysed."

"With no-one of her own, poor soul."

"No-one as really cared."

"Barring them children of her sister's."

"And them not so young as they were, by the look of it."

"None too many of them has showed up today, mind."

"They were pleased enough to come down here during the bombing. When their Mother brought them down from Bristol."

"When the steam trains were still running . . ."

"Do you remember all them kids ? Marching up from the station . . ."

"Vacuees, they were. From the Bristol Blitz. Oh-ah - I never knew how Miss Petherton fitted them all in, and her sister and all."

"It's not the same, mind. Nieces and nephews. Not like your own."

"Aye - the poor soul had nobody."

"She had me," Rosemary said, turning on the little string of villagers at the tail of the procession. "Who do you think was with her at the last ? She was as dear to me as my own mother, Aunt Mary was." And taking old Charlie's hand she helped him through the snicket and into the Churchyard.

"No offence meant, my dear."

"To be honest, I didn't know you, love. Didn't recognise you. You being that much younger than all the rest of them."

"And that much livelier and all."

"And dressed so cheerful."

Well, I don't feel that lively right now, Rosemary thought, realising she'd all but gone clockwise round the bloody roundabout. Time for a break. And she pulled in at a café with a pink and white striped awning, and tubs of geraniums outside on the pavement. God almighty ! That was a near thing. And just when I thought I was doing so nicely.

"Café au lait, s'il vous plaît, Mam'selle."

9

She sat out under the awning. And checked her position on the map. Not bad. Four hours behind her, and she was probably half way there. Good going, considering.

"Considering !" Edward would have pulled her up sharp. "Considering *what*, darling ?"

Considering the fact that I've never driven in France before, dear boy, she would answer him now. Not without a touch of sarcasm. Considering that I've no-one with me to navigate or share the driving.

Edward can be a pain, she admitted. Reluctant as she still was to malign him. A pedantic pain.

She felt better for the break, bowling along now with the window down. Never mind the noise, the dust. At least she wouldn't fry.

On either side, as far as the eye could see, were vast fields of the same crop. Miles and miles of it. Well, kilometres, to be precise. She couldn't identify it as she sped by. With the sun high in the sky, she pulled onto the wide grass verge and found a shady spot for her picnic. And now at close quarters she recognised the blanketing crop. Sweetcorn. That's it, of course. Down here, a good hour's drive into the cornbelt, the first featheriness was clearly sprouting.

Sweetcorn, she thought, with that once familiar mixture of fear, anticipation, and disgust. Sweetcorn.

Dad had grown sweetcorn one year on the allotment. Quite an exotic vegetable for him. Four full rows he'd planted, and it had done well. It had been Rosemary's job to water the sweetcorn. Last thing before bed.

"Have you been over to the allotment yet ?"

"Not yet, Dad. But I'm in the middle of my homework. Can't I do it later ?"

"Later ! Later ! Do as you're told, and do it at once. I shall be over in a minute to check. Go on. Now !"

Quick, quick, then. Before he got down there. Leave the Algebra. Out of the gate. Across the street. Down the lane and over the footbridge to the allotments. With any luck there would still be other people around, weeding, watering, inspecting their plots. With any luck . . .

Get the watering can from the shed. Fill it from the tap by the gate. Lug it - the cumbersome thing - back to Dad's patch. It usually meant ten or twelve to water the sweetcorn properly. The hose wasn't long enough to reach the sweetcorn bed.

And I must have watered it properly, Rosemary thought grimly, looking back. It grew incredibly tall and strong that summer. Dad's sweetcorn certainly was as high as an elephant's eye. And not a baby elephant either. Like a jungle it was, our sweetcorn bed that long ago summer.

Rosemary shuddered, bowling along the French motorway this scorching afternoon. Remembering the ritual. How Dad would come to check she wasn't skimping. No matter how fast she worked, he always arrived before she had finished. How he'd call her into the shed. Shutting out any of the other allotment holders who were still there. Shutting out the evening sunlight. The real world. How he'd push her down among the sacks, the bags of John Innes and fine sand, among the jumble of rakes and spades and hoes. How he'd . . .

But no, she wouldn't, she mustn't think about all that. It was finished and done with long ago. Father was dead. Mother was dead. And Rosemary had survived Dad and his bloody games. She had survived.

The landscape was changing now, and with it the crop. Apart from the odd vineyard, the odd smallholding with neat rows of beans and tomatoes, a goat perhaps, a few chickens scratching in the dust, Rosemary was driving through a grey-green landscape. Reaching to every horizon were fields of the one crop. A tall plant, with large leaves. But this time, she could not identify it.

She drove on. Through villages and towns. Through a city with a balustraded bridge across a wide clear river. And on and on, with the shadows lengthening to her left as she came off the motorway, off the A road, and at last saw the signpost she was looking for : ST JUSTE SUR CHARENTE.

Now to find the gîte.

* * *

11

Chapter Three

Hoping that she was on the right track, Rosemary drew up at the gate of a farmstead standing alone above the lush river valley, a good mile from any other building.

A couple of weeks ago, the day before she had been called down to Somerset to look after Aunt Mary, a sketch map had arrived from St Juste along with confirmation of their booking and various other bits of information.

"I say, Rosie," she remembered Edward's excitement now. With a momentary pang. "There's a chateau, look. A *vallée verte*, whatever that might be. A swimming pool."

"We're a fair distance out of the village, aren't we. And isolated."

A springer spaniel, liver and white, jumped down from look-out duty on the wood pile, and barking madly went and nudged her master, a man in his late fifties by the look of it, in denim overalls and the regulation black beret, who was attacking the unruly patch of grass between the barn and the farm house with an asthmatic mower, and had not heard the car.

"Excusez, Monsieur," Rosemary called to him, "but I'm looking for . . ."

"Ah, Madame ! Vous êtes bien arrivez. It is me you are looking for, I think."

"Monsieur Forêt ?"

"Oui, oui. I was just tidying up for you," he explained, indicating the lawn. "While I waited."

And opening the gate, he guided Rosemary into the yard and showed her where to park among the neatly stacked logs and the bales of straw in the rickety timber-framed barn which completely filled that side of the farmyard. It was open to the elements at the front where the low-slung pantiled roof was supported on five gigantic tree trunks that could well have been in place since the days of Joan of Arc.

"You are alone, Madame ?"

She realised that she had switched quite painlessly into French. After all these years, not only did she understand Monsieur Forêt without difficulty. But, much more surprisingly, he appeared to be understanding her as well.

"Well, um, there was a hitch. My, er, husband will be joining me in a day or two."

Stupid of her. Why on earth should she lie to him ? As if her solitary state was shameful or pathetic. As if it were a matter of self-respect. Having, or not having, a companion, a friend, a lover. A man in her life.

"Eh, bien . . ." Rosemary had a disconcerting suspicion that Mr Forêt understood the situation. Understood it perfectly. " . . . let me show you the house."

"This is it, then ? But this - this must be the farmhouse, surely. Your farmhouse."

"This is your gîte, Madame, yes. And it is the farmhouse, of course. We lived here ourselves until recently when we moved into a modern apartment in the town. More convenient for my wife. But my family has lived here in this old house for . . ." and he spread his arms expressively, "for generations."

The back door (the only door) opened straight into a large square kitchen, with a flagged floor, a beamed ceiling. There were three small windows set low in the thick walls, one beside the cream pottery sink with a view across the farmyard and away to the wooded valley below.

The hearth took up practically the length of one wall : a stone ledge with fire-dogs under a blackened canopy to draw the smoke up into the four-foot-square chimney. With a pile of logs this side, a pile of kindling that. For a mantelpiece there was a heavy oak beam, knotted and scorched, from which were hanging an assortment of pots and pans, ladles and sieves, bunches of dried herbs, and other unidentifiable objects.

"Do I cook on the fire, Monsieur ?"

But he laughed, and putting a hand on her shoulder pointed her towards a gas cooker beside the sink. "Camping gas," he explained. "But you are welcome to light the fire any time. No shortage of wood. You saw the barn. I'll chop more whenever you need it. Just let me know, OK ?"

In the middle of the room was a solid table, large enough to seat a family of ten. It was covered with a red-and-white checked oilcloth, very French, that matched the frilly gingham curtains.

13

And six ladder-back chairs with worn rush seats. The only other item of furniture was a slightly lop-sided dresser with blue and white china set out neatly on its shelves - plates, bowls, tureens.

"It's . . . it's simply heavenly," Rosemary told him, scarcely able to wait to light the fire, put a jug of wild flowers on the table, and make it her own.

"Mind the step," he warned, taking her through to the astonishing sittingroom which was high like a medieval hall. Stairs in the corner led up to a minstrels' gallery no less, supported on three hefty tree trunks all knobbly with knots and the stumps of branches. The floor in here was of quarry tiles in a dull burnt sienna, with a couple of rag rugs beside the uncomfortably formal sofa.

"Oh, Monsieur . . . !"

"You have of course the TV," Mr Forêt showed her with pride. "And," throwing open a door under the stairs, "all the mod cons, as I told you in my letter."

Sure enough, there was a sparkling modern bathroom. It had a new un-used look to it and seemed decidedly out of place, with its tasteful blue bath, bidet, shower and - thank God - a proper flush loo.

"Better to pay a bit more and be certain of decent plumbing," Edward had said, the night they were going through the brochure, *Self-Catering Holidays in France*, choosing their gîte. "Couldn't face a bucket in a shed."

"And now, en haut," Mr Forêt said, leading the way up the steep and rather rickety stairs.

Apart from the railed gallery on which there was nothing except an enormous elaborately carved wardrobe, there were two good bedrooms above the kitchen. One with modern twin divans, the other all but filled by a vast bedstead billowing with feather duvets and plump pillows.

"This we found impossible to dismantle when we moved to the flat," said Mr Forêt. "As you see, it is here to stay."

"But how does anyone get into it ?" Rosemary spluttered, taking a running jump at the breast-high bed, and collapsing against it defeated.

"Voilà !" And from under the bedstead, he pulled out a mahogany mounting block. He gave her his hand, and ascending regally, she perched aloft while he explained about window catches, extra bedding.

"In spite of what it says in the contract," he told her, "I do provide the linen for this old bed. I doubt whether my visitors would bring anything large enough to fit. My sister has helped me to make it up today, in case you chose to sleep in here."

"Oh, yes please - I've never seen such a bed. And real linen to go with it. Thank you."

"I'll just help you unload the car. Then I must be off home."

"I'll manage the rest," she said, when most of her stuff was stacked in the kitchen. "Your dog seems to be telling you she's had enough, I think." And Rosemary crouched down to fondle the spaniel's silky ears.

"Erna !" he called softly, and the dog slunk guiltily across to her master, nudging his hand until he gave her a reassuring pat. "If you start to pet her, she'll not give you a minute's peace."

"Oh, I know what you mean," Rosemary said, thinking of Lucy, Aunt Mary's faithful old labrador, her childhood friend and confidant.

"Be sure to let me know if there's anything else you need," he told her as he put on his bicycle clips. "Anything I've forgotten." And with a half-apologetic smile, "You are in fact my first tenant, Madame. You are, what shall we say, my guinea-pig."

It was dark by the time Rosemary was sorted out.

"For heaven's sake, Ma !" Betsy had said helping to load the last bits and pieces into the car on Friday morning. *Yesterday* morning. "It's only for a fortnight, isn't it ? Good job I'm not coming with you. I can see I'd have ended up strapped to the roof rack. Or running along behind."

Suddenly she felt hungry. Ravenously hungry. She'd leave the rest of the unpacking till later. Pop into St Juste now before everything closed. And tonight, maybe she'd eat out. It was a fair sized place, a small town rather than a village. There'd be three or four restaurants for sure.

She tidied herself up, and locking the back door, Rosemary peeped in at her own window, savouring the cosiness of lamplight on checked gingham. The uneven flagstones shiny from the footsteps of Mr Forêt's ancestors, not to mention centuries of energetic scrubbing.

15

It gave her the same acute pleasure she suddenly remembered feeling on that long-ago birthday. When she'd been given the dolls house. Her sixth ? Her fifth birthday. That would be it - just before she started school.

"We never had a dolls house," Rosie's big sister Maggie had grumbled. On the birthday morning. "She seems to get everything, spoilt brat !"

"Now then, Maggie, love," Mother had said gently. "Don't let's have any of that today. Not on her birthday. Be fair. Please."

"Fair ! It's not in the least bit fair ! Did we ever have a dolls house, any of us ? Me ? Frances or Kate ? None of us had a dolls house. But Rosie, darling Rosie, she gets one. Of course she does."

"Maggie ! What would you want with a dolls house, for heaven's sake ? At your age ? A dolls house, indeed !"

"I don't want one *now*, do I. I wanted it *then*. When I was her age."

"But it was war time, love. No-one had a dolls house then. It wasn't anybody's fault. It was the war."

"Well, it's still not fair. Nobody understood me then. Nobody understands me now."

And grown-up Maggie, wearing under her navy gym-slip her first bra, big sister Maggie rushed off to school in a flood of angry tears.

"Why is she always cross with me, our Maggie ?" the five year old Rosie had asked, setting her birthday cards out around her porridge bowl as Mother cleared the table.

"Pay no attention," Mother had said, fetching herself another cup of tea from the big brown pot on the range. "She's at a difficult age. She doesn't mean half she says. Let you and me set everything out nice and neat for the dolls house family, should we ? Now they've all got off to school, the others."

What a beautiful dolls house it had been. From the posh Toy Shop in the Square. It had been in the window for weeks. Rosemary had been pressing her nose to the plate-glass and staring at it in wonder every time they went by to the Co-op, she and Mother.

And today, Rosie's Fifth Birthday, the dolls house had been there beside her bed when she woke up.

"Turn your head away ! Shut your eyes !" Maggie had yelled at her, as she struggled to do up her new Size Ten cotton bra in front of the mirror. "Don't you dare look till I've got my vest on. You little brat, you !"

Maggie had forgotten about the Birthday.

What a beautiful dolls house. There were four rooms, and a bathroom in the attic. It had carpets and wallpaper. And lights that really switched on and off. When the family were all asleep in their beds you could close the front so that everything was safe and snug.

"There should be five children and a baby in the dolls house," her brother Davy had said when he came in at teatime after doing his paper round. He must have been twelve at the time, the nearest to Rosemary in age. "Five kids and a baby. Like us."

"I'm not a baby !" The middle-aged artist in this isolated French farmyard remembered her infant indignation vividly. "I'll be going to school soon. I'm not a baby."

"You're *our* baby, stupid. The baby of the family. Come on, see what I've got you for your birthday." And from the pocket of his grey flannel shorts he had produced a knobbly parcel.

"Oh, Davy !" There, curled up in a tiny basket was a tabby cat, dolls house sized. And a friendly brown and white spaniel to go with it.

"Families need pets," young Davy had told her solemnly, trying to disguise his delight at her delight. "When I grow up I shall have a dog, an Alsatian. And two cats. And mice and rabbits. No matter what Dad says. You just see if I don't !"

"Can we leave the lights on, Mummy ?" she'd begged when she was tucked up in bed that night. "You know. In the dolls house. Please. *Please*."

"Well, the batteries won't last long. I can't keep buying new ones."

"Oh, please."

"Just this once, then. As it's your birthday. One of us will switch them off later when you're asleep. There ! How's that ?"

"Oh, isn't it pretty. It's the absolutely best dolls house in the whole world."

"Night-night, then. My little lamb."

"But I'm a big girl now, Mummy . . ."

"You'll always be my little lamb. No matter what."

And Rosie was alone. At last. Alone with her treasure.

Very quietly she climbed out of bed and tip-toeing across the lino she lay on her tummy on the woolly mat by the fireplace. Then with the most intense pleasure she'd ever known she peeped into the lighted windows of the dolls house. At the children asleep upstairs in their bunks. At the baby in its white cot. At Mother making a cup of tea in the kitchen, the cat purring contentedly in his basket beside the range. At Father sitting dozing over the evening paper by the sittingroom fire, with the family dog at his feet.

"Out of bed ?" Dad had crept into the room without little Rosie hearing him. "Naughty girl !"

Instinctively she jumped back into bed, pulling her nightie as far down as it would go, and the eiderdown right up to her nose.

"Don't I get a goodnight kiss, then ? A birthday kiss ? It's not every Daddy buys such a beautiful present for his little girlie."

Rosie froze, her legs clamped tight together. Her nightie she anchored desperately between her toes. "Thank you, Daddy. It is a lovely dolls house. A really lovely dolls house."

"Is that all I'm going to get then ? I think I deserve a proper kiss tonight. One of our Special Secret Kisses. Don't you ?" And crouching down beside the bed . . .

"No ! No ! Not on my birthday, Daddy ! Not again - please !"

. . . Dad slid his hand down between the sheets.

"There. There's my little sweetheart," he groaned. "Daddy's little princess."

"No ! Please ! Not tonight, not again, Daddy ! Not on my birthday !" At last she got the words out.

Rosemary's cries set up a cackling of alarm in Mr Forêt's hen-house. And below her somewhere in the woods along the vallée verte a dog, a dog fox perhaps, howled for his mate.

Shit !

She shook herself angrily. She'd thought she was over all that. Choking back the wisps of that almost forgotten horror, Rosemary turned away from the softly-lit dolls house window, and stumbled across to the Morris Minor in the barn.

* * *

18

Chapter Four

Although it was well after nine o'clock by then, Bon Marché the Hypermarket, was still busy when Rosemary found it. And there was still bread on the shelves - warm crusty baguettes, three foot long and smelling delicious. With brie and tomatoes, coffee beans, and a bottle of Bordeaux she could survive quite happily, but nevertheless this evening she would treat herself to a meal out. To celebrate.

There were several possibilities on La Place de Ville, cafés with tables set out on the cobbles under the sweet-smelling lime trees. Reluctant to intrude on any of the lively family parties outside, Rosemary ventured a trifle self-consciously into the nearest establishment, Le Coq d'Or, and instinctively made for a small table in the corner.

"Mais non, Madame !" The proprietor, a tall gangly man with a mop of tight grey curls, intercepted her, inviting her with a flourish to share the large table at the window where he and his assistant were at supper. There was nobody else indoors.

"That's more like it," he said, as she settled herself on the bench opposite them. "Pierre - the wine !"

Pierre, a slight baby-faced youth, whose heavily tattooed arms were exposed rather alarmingly by the black sleeveless vest under his Persil-white apron, poured Rosemary a glass of red wine, re-filling the other two glasses at the same time, and then fetched another bottle from behind the bar.

"Now Madame, what can we offer you?" asked the older man.

For a start, they insisted she should share their platter of cruditées. Then, guided by Anton, patron and chef it seemed, she chose chicken in a rich garlic sauce, the camembert, raspberry sorbet.

"Vin de pays," Anton explained as he filled their glasses yet again. "The very best."

The wine was indeed working wonders. Rosemary was all aglow, warmed by the wine, the air of carnival outside in the square, the easy cameraderie around the table.

"You are staying in these parts, Madame ?"

"I've taken a cottage, a farmhouse really, for a fortnight."

"Eh, bien - La Maison Forêt ? I heard that Hugo was expecting visitors from England. But you are alone, Madame ?"

"Not exactly." She'd actually forgotten about Edward. Forgotten the pain. She must stock up with this excellent wine. For the bad moments. "My, er, husband will be joining me any day." Again, the lie. But not much sense in letting the whole world know I'm up there by myself, she reasoned.

Outside, the family groups were breaking up as people drifted off home. Some of them, coming in to pay their bills, settled round the big table for coffee and cognac. With her place already established, Rosemary found herself drawn painlessly into the late night banter. And again, to her surprise, she realised she was perfectly at home with the language. Must be like cycling, she thought. Once mastered, never forgotten. And come to think of it, she had shown quite a flair for French at school.

Yes. Oral French with, er - Mamoiselle le Brun. On those far off Fifth Form Friday afternoons.

"Alors, mes enfants - who will translate the first paragraph for us ? No, not you Rosemary. Let's give the others a chance, shall we ?"

A small triumph that. In her otherwise undistinguished school career. That Mamoiselle le Brun, this thin shabby exile from France who had chosen to stay on to meet the daily challenge of the classroom after the war, should have such faith in Rosemary's gift for French. And still after all these years . . . extraordinary !

The coffee pot was circulating again.

"No. No more for me, thank you. I really must be going."

"You will come and eat with us again," Anton insisted warmly as he counted out her change. "I shall be looking out for you. And next time you must try our snails. So delicious, believe me. You will see. Bon nuit, bon nuit, Madame."

The road to the farm was pitch black, so far from the lights of the village. She was glad of the welcome glow from the kitchen windows as she got out to open the heavy gate.

Unloading the groceries from the car, she noticed among one or two items that she had overlooked earlier, the wooden box. Aunt Mary's wooden box. It took Rosemary a moment to identify it.

How the hell had she come to bring it to France with her ? This last mysterious gift from Aunt Mary. This sturdy wooden box that judging from the picture on the lid appeared to contain children's bricks. For Heaven's sake ! Multi-coloured wooden building blocks. The sort that would have had a place in every Edwardian nursery. And yet it was obviously something very special, very precious to Aunt Mary who had gone to such lengths, paralysed and speechless as she had been by then, to ensure that Rosemary found the box. To ensure that Rosemary understood that the box and whatever it contained was for her.

Carrying it into the kitchen of Mr Forêt's farmhouse now, Rosemary was back in Isle St Agnes. At Aunt Mary's bedside. That last morning.

Ben Philips, the Isle St Agnes GP had phoned Rosemary a few days before, on the Sunday. Two weeks ago ? Two short weeks.

"Your Aunt's had a stroke, Rosie. Can you come over?"

They had been at school together, Ben and Rosemary, though he was a year ahead of her. She'd had a crush on him right through the Upper School. Ben had been a high flyer, going up to Edinburgh to do Medicine, while Rosemary had only just scraped into Art College.

"Poor old love, poor Aunt Mary - is it serious, Ben ?"

"'Fraid so. She could hang on for a few days. She's always been such a fighter, your Aunt Mary. But there's not much hope."

"I'll come down. I'll come straight away."

"Bless you, Rosie. As you know, she's always insisted that if anything like this should happen, she wanted to die in her own bed."

"Don't you go carting me off to Taunton, young man," he remembered her saying. "I want none of these devilish tricks they get up to nowadays. None of your transplants, thank you. None of your resuscitation just when I'm drifting away. When the time comes, let me die peacefully in my own bed. Right ? And send for Rosemary. None of the rest of them, mind. It's my Rosie I want beside me at the end."

"She's said the same to me, Ben. More than once over the years. Look, I'll set off as soon as the others come in. Betsy and Miranda. They popped over to the pub for a quick drink with Edward. My Edward - you know. While I made the gravy. They won't be many minutes. I can't set off till they get back. I'm looking after the baby for Miranda. Young Tommy. I should be down there by four o'clock easily. Will she be all right till then ?"

"Yes. Yes, I fetched old Charlie Taylor to sit with her. There he is holding her hand and, by the look of it, at last finding the words he's been searching for all these years. I'd better warn you, she's completely helpless. No speech either. It might be a bit of a shock for you . . ."

"Don't worry, Ben. Mother was in a pretty poor way at the end. I'll cope. But thanks for preparing me."

"You're a great girl, Rosie. I felt sure you'd come. I've got a strong suspicion that she's willing herself to hang on until you get here, the old battle-axe."

The road was clear, fortunately, and Rosemary made it inside two hours. Aunt Mary recognised her when she reached her bedside. There was indeed a gleam of battle in the old girl's eyes as she lay there shattered, helpless as a baby.

"I could organise a night nurse," Ben offered before leaving the two of them alone. "Don't want you cracking up, do we."

"No," she told him firmly. "Aunt Mary has been like a second mother to me. Closer than Mother in many ways. She wouldn't want strangers fussing her. Not while I can cope."

"Well, tell me the minute it begins to get too much for you. And in the meantime, I'll pop in whenever I'm passing."

Rosemary made Aunt Mary as comfortable as possible. She changed her soiled nappy. Washed her tenderly with a bar of luxurious soap she'd unearthed in the bathroom cabinet.

"Mm - that smells good," she said, easing her aunt's clenched limbs into a nice clean nightie.

"A good job this happened now," she said later. "Two weeks time and I'd have been over in France. Then what, eh ?"

Having failed to persuade Aunt Mary to taste the insipid mush that Ben had left for her, Rosemary poured herself a whisky and settled down in the pool of light from the reading lamp by the sick bed. And taking her aunt's useless hand in her own, she began to talk quietly about the memories they shared.

"Remember the time . . . ?

" . . . the time you took us all down to Weymouth ? Just after the war, it must have been. My first sight of the sea. At last I discovered where the train went to after we'd got off here. Remember ?

" . . . the time I spent the whole summer with you, after I'd had the measles and they sent me down here to recuperate. The whole summer we had together. Remember ?

" . . . the time, oh Lord ! - the time they found I'd been shop-lifting with that rough lot from the Council Houses. And instead of punishing me as Father intended, you took me off to Scotland, just the two of us, touring through the Highlands in that sports car you were so proud of. Treating me like a grown-up. Staying in proper hotels and that. Looking back, I guess that's when I started to paint. Remember ?"

But Aunt Mary slept.

Lifting the withered hand tenderly back into bed, Rosemary slipped out of the room. When she'd phoned Betsy to let her know how things were, she crept back to her post with her glass topped up and a slim volume of poetry which she settled down to read.

A slight noise from the bed, nothing more than a shapeless gurgle, drew Rosemary's eyes to her Aunt's. In spite of the devastation the stroke had inflicted on her, it was clear the old dear had her wits about her still.

Understanding the signal immediately, Rosemary began to read aloud from the book in her hands : '*First Impressions*, a collection of the poetry of Mary Petherton', her Aunt Mary, that had come out to considerable acclaim before Rosemary herself was even thought of. Way back in the thirties.

"**My grief was brief**," Rosemary read with a lump in her throat, "**so have no fears for future fraught encounters, bathed in tears**."

Now and again, as her poems were read out, Aunt Mary managed a twisted dribbling signal of appreciation. Not quite a smile, but a signal nevertheless.

The days had passed peacefully in Orchard Cottage. Even happily. Those last few days. There was no noticeable change in Aunt Mary's condition, either for better or for worse. Ben called in every day. Sometimes more than once. His wife, Kitty, looked in a couple of times, first with a slice of rhubarb pie, another time with a small earthenware casserole of rabbit for her supper.

"Mm - that was so delicious, Kitty. Thank you. It reminds me of the wonderful dinners Aunt Mary used to make us. Delicious."

"It's your Aunt Mary's recipe actually," Kitty told her. "It's the rosemary that reminds you. Rosemary, as the poet said : that's for remembrance."

Old Charlie came too, to sit holding the senseless hand of his stricken sweetheart while Rosemary snatched an hour's sleep, or had a bath, or drove into the village for a bit of shopping. Bread, stamps, Lucozade, flowers for the sick room.

Monday, Tuesday, Wednesday, Thursday . . .

On the Friday morning, clean and fed and comfortable as Rosemary knew she was, Aunt Mary seemed to grow agitated.

"Oh, lovey - what's the matter ? What is it you're trying to tell me ?" It was distressing to see the vain efforts the poor soul was making to speak. Afterwards, thinking about it, Rosemary wondered whether it was by pure telepathy that Aunt Mary had communicated with her that morning. A last supreme effort of will.

Somehow, miraculously almost, Aunt Mary guided her niece to the built-in wardrobe beside the chimney breast in her bedroom. With grunts and gurgles and frantic eye signals, she then guided Rosemary to a battered leather suitcase on the top shelf buried beneath a pile of straw hats and old handbags.

Setting it down on Aunt Mary's bed, Rosemary wiped the dust from the top of the case with the damp flannel on the wash basin, and with intense curiosity, matched only by the excitement in the eyes of the woman in the bed, she clicked back the catches.

The case was locked.

Without any need for guidance here, remembering Aunt Mary's life-long habit with keys, Rosemary rushed down stairs to the sittingroom, and opening the door of the grandfather clock she scrabbled around inside it. Sure enough, there were a dozen keys of all shapes and sizes hanging from nails knocked higgledy-piggledy into the clock case. Gathering them all up, she ran back to her aunt's bedroom.

Aunt Mary was lying there with wild eyes now, panting and dribbling, her breath rattling in her throat.

"Here ! I've found them. Is it one of these ?" Rosemary babbled desperately as she tried one key after another. "Yes! Here we are - this one fits. There !"

Heaven knows what she was expecting to find after all this. Letters probably, though the box was heavy. A bundle of yellowing love letters tied up with ribbon. Diaries. The Will. But certainly not this.

24

Inside the suitcase was a large-ish flat-ish wooden box. Judging from the picture on the lid it was a box of children's wooden building bricks. Perhaps a cherished memento from Aunt Mary's nursery days between the Victorians and the First World War.

Mystified, wondering whether in fact Aunt Mary's mind had gone with her poor body, Rosemary lifted the wooden box out onto the bed. But before she could open the sliding lid Aunt Mary made one more effort to communicate.

"Yours," she said quite plainly. "Yours, Rosie."

And then she died.

With all the hoo-ha, the funeral arrangements and so on, there had not been a chance to inspect the contents of Aunt Mary's mysterious parting gift. Not then. Not since. Indeed it was a wonder Rosemary had remembered to gather the thing up with the other bits and pieces, mainly house plants, that she took with her when she eventually locked up her aunt's cottage (Rosemary's cottage, lock, stock and barrel, once probate had gone through) and set off for home.

I'll have to get my skates on, she remembered thinking, driving up to her own front door on Wednesday evening. There's only tomorrow. Before we leave for France. Edward and I. And so much to be done. I hope he's seen to the travellers cheques and all. The insurance. So many last minute things to think of.

"Oh, Ma !" Betsy had hugged her close and protective, coming out to greet her. "Oh, Ma - it's Edward. He's gone off with Miranda."

Rosemary had been stunned. As if Betsy had delivered a karate chop to the back of her neck.

"Come on. Come on in, Ma. I'll see to all this later." And she locked the car door and helped her mother into the house. "Have a drink. Have a bath. Go on, have a bath. I'll come and talk to you while you soak. I'll bring you a whisky. Oh, Ma - how could he !"

Lying in the comforting bubbles, a glass on the soap-rack, Betsy squatting on the loo with her Rum and Black, Rosemary felt stronger.

"Go on, then. Tell me."

"Well, I kind-of knew something had been going on ever since you went over to Somerset."

"Why didn't you tell me, then ? Why didn't you tell me yesterday ?" When Betsy was over for the funeral.

"You had enough on your plate yesterday, Ma. In any case, I didn't know *what* was going on, did I? Didn't know it was Edward. Miranda was out a lot. Always asking me to baby-sit. And she was being a bit mysterious I noticed. Not very forthcoming. You know. When I look back, I guess it was pretty obvious. I just wasn't thinking along those lines."

They each had a slurp from their glasses as if to give them courage.

"She kept asking when you'd be back. I think she was expecting you to come home last night. Right after the funeral. She was pretty funny with me. Kind of aggressive. Anyway, when I told her you'd be home today, she began gathering up her stuff. It's quite a relief to have the house back to normal, I must admit. All her bloody herbs and fleeces. That awful smell of boiling wool. Not to mention Tommy's rubbish. The toys, the damp nappies everywhere, the permanent goo on the high chair . . ."

"Yes, yes. Get on with it, girl."

"Right. Where was I? Oh, yes - last night. Well, last night, as you know, I was going up to London to meet Steve. He'd got us tickets for Scream and Shout, hadn't he. That's why I rushed off from Aunt Mary's party without saying much. OK?"

"I'd forgotten. You can tell me about it later. But get on with it now. The bath's getting cold."

"Ah! Don't leap out on me. Please not that, Ma! Middle-aged flesh is so disgusting."

"Just finish the bloody story, girl." Rosemary ran some more hot into the bath.

"OK - OK - I'm doing my best."

"OK!"

"Yes, well, I stayed up in London with Steve over night. We went to the flat. A couple of the girls are still there, staying up over Easter. So we had quite a whacky time."

"Betsy!"

"And when I got back this morning they'd gone."

"Gone?"

"Yes. They'd gone. Miranda. Tommy. All her wool and that. All the nappies off the airer. They'd clean gone."

"But how do you know they've gone to Edward, love? She was

always a bit of a gypsy, Miranda. Look how she landed on us. She could have gone anywhere."

"'Fraid not, Ma. She's gone to Edward all right. I found a note. She'd left it by the tea caddy. Here - look for yourself."

"I haven't got my bloody glasses, have I. Read it to me."

"Brace yourself then. Have a sip of the old whatsit. Right, here goes : '**Betsy** . . . ' No DEAR mind. Just plain Betsy. After all the hours I've devoted to that damn kid of hers."

"Oh, come on, can't you. What does she say ?"

" '**Betsy - tell your mother we're moving in with Edward. Yes, _her_ Edward. Sorry, but it just happened that way. Thanks for everything. Miranda.**' "

What a sod, Rosemary thought now in the kitchen of Mr Forêt's farmhouse in deepest France. What a fucking sod. Edward. How could he ? When I'd thought that for once we'd found something, well - something special. Permanent and special.

Oh, bugger the pair of them, she told herself bitterly. I'm not going to let them spoil this and all.

And by way of distraction, she took Aunt Mary's wooden box, cleared a space for it among the groceries on the red and white oil-cloth, and without more ado, firmly and purposefully, Rosemary slid open the close-fitting lid.

* * *

27

Chapter Five

In spite of the long day she had had, Rosemary was unable to sleep. Was it only this morning that she had set out from Lisieux ? Only yesterday she'd crossed from Portsmouth to Le Havre ?

She switched on the reading light, and crawling to the edge of the bed, felt for the mounting block with her bare toes.

What an extraordinary thing that Aunt Mary should have had that box and its contents all these years. Hidden away. Why had it never been brought out ? During Rosemary's own childhood. Or later on, when she had taken Billy and Betsy, her own kids, to visit their Great Aunt Mary. How was it, why was it, that through all the holidays in Isle St Agnes, all the wet afternoons in Orchard Cottage, all the winter evenings round the peat fire, Rosemary had neither seen nor heard of the wooden box and its mysterious contents ? Very odd.

Collecting the brick-box from the window sill where she'd left it at bedtime, she scrambled up again under the feather quilt in its starched linen cover.

And now again she slid open the tight-fitting lid. The lid with the picture on it of a Toy Town castle made from brightly coloured wooden building blocks. Cubes and pillars, beams and arches in a variety of sizes. And again, as she had been earlier in Mr Forêt's kitchen, she was amazed at what the box contained.

Nestling in yellowing tissue paper was a set of wooden skittles. Nine-pins. Nine little mannikins, in fact. Each of them beautifully carved and lovingly painted. Each one different from its fellows. Each, the little figure of a man. The set was a work of art. No question about that.

Taking them out of their wrappings, spreading them around her on the quilt, she studied them carefully, one by one. They were carved with great delicacy. Painted with an earthy gusto. In the various expressions on their little wooden faces there was a primitive vitality. The rich colours the artist had used - clear blue, dull pinky-red, dark green, white, gold, black - reminded Rosemary of . . .

And suddenly, there she was in the old squat Church dedicated to St Agnes, on the edge of the Somerset Levels.

Standing on a plump hassock Rosie could just see over the top of the pew in front. She was in her Sunday dress, though it didn't feel like Sunday. The yellow dress with tiny daisies scattered all over it and a skirt that swirled out around her as she skipped across the orchard with the others. The church bells summoning them so insistently.

And everyone was in Church with her, she remembered. Mummy and Henry. Frances and Kate and Maggie. And Davy running his Dinky car along the ledge for the hymn books till Aunt Mary gave him a look. All of them were together. Except Father, of course. Father never went with them to Somerset. Not ever.

The sun was shining through the stained glass windows and throwing rainbow patterns on the floor. She could see them still. Dancing rainbows that caught in people's hats and hair and lit up their faces as they sang.

"Oh God our help in ages past . . ."

When the singing stopped the Church bells started up again. Ringing and ringing.

"Davy ! Davy, listen ! What is it ?"

She had been woken by bells that same long ago morning. Bells that filled the air with excitement. That flavoured their porridge. That called urgently to them as they processed across the orchard and through the snicket into the churchyard. And the grass still wet with dew as the child in the yellow dress danced along among the fading apple blossom.

"Oh, look at her, Mother ! She's getting her sandals soaked. Keep to the path, Rosie, for heaven's sake."

"Don't fuss so, Maggie," Mother had chided. "What does it matter. Let her be, can't you."

Everybody in the world must have been in Church that morning. There were people crowded round the font, perched on cold radiators, propping themselves up against the Fitzwilliam tomb where Sir Gawain and Lady Lucy had lain in effigy since the time of the Crusades, as Davy was to tell her later, their twelve children kneeling around them.

Mummy was crying, little Rosie realised with a shock. And others were too. Grown-ups dabbing their eyes as the Vicar read out a long list of names.

" . . . David Webster, Roy Wilks, William Wilks, Andrew Woodseaves . . ."

Rosie clambered up onto the seat, put her thumb in her mouth, her index finger comfortingly on her nose, and lent against Aunt Mary.

" . . . Edward Yandle, Eric Yattendon, James Yeo."

Aunt Mary put an arm round her and cuddled her tight.

" . . . for these thy children who have laid down their lives for their country . . ."

And it was then, as the Vicar droned on and on, then that Rosie had first spotted the carved figures around the pulpit.

"I don't believe you," Margaret had said years later when the talk had been about earliest memories. "You weren't much more than a toddler when the War ended. You were scarcely three years old. I was only twelve myself. You can't possibly remember. You always tell such stories."

But Rosie did remember. Then. And now. She remembered it all vividly. The tears. The sunshine. The voice of the Vicar reading out the names. The rainbow patterns on the floor.

She remembered too her first startling recognition that among the jumble of carving around the pulpit were figures and faces. Human figures. Human faces.

"It was the artist in you, Rosie," Edward had suggested, the time she had taken him down to meet Aunt Mary. When she'd shown him round the Church. "The embryonic artist in you."

"Oh, come on - I was no more than a toddler."

Over the years, she had come to know all the carvings, of course. At College she had done a special study of them for her Diploma : the wooden figures on the roof bosses, the stone figures on the rood screen, the marble figures on the tombs. The solemn faces, the wicked ones, the laughing ones. Faithful portraits, no doubt, of the saints and sinners of this isolated community. Portraits that had miraculously escaped the ravages of time, and Cromwell's men.

And all of these faces she remembered washed in the shifting colours of the Great East Window for which Isle St Agnes is justly famous. The same colours, she now realised, as were captured in the delicately painted detail on the nine little figures spread out around her on the crisp French quilt.

30

There must be a connection.

Someone from the village must have made the set of nine-pins. Carving them and colouring them for Aunt Mary. Old Charlie, perhaps. Or one of her other beaux. That must be it. For much as they resembled the medieval figures in the distant Somerset church, the skittles had a modern feel about them. Modern-ish. They were certainly not as old as the Edwardian brick box in which they had been kept. She felt sure of that.

Who had made them ? And why ? And, most intriguing of all, as she was to inherit everything of Aunt Mary's - cottage and contents - why the urgency to ensure that Rosemary found them in those last few minutes before the old lady died ?

The questions swirled around in her head. A head already confused by Mr Anton's generosity with the local vin de pays. She must leave it for tonight. Puzzle it out in the morning.

One by one, she stood the brightly painted figures up in their box. Then kneeling at the foot of the bed, she reached up and balanced the box on the beam where she could see them, her nine little mannikins as she snuggled down among the pillows.

And as she switched off the bedside light this time, she saw that dawn was breaking across Mr Forêt's fields. His fields of young sunflowers.

* * *

Chapter Six

It was late when Rosemary woke next morning. Indeed she might have slept all day if Mr Forêt had not come up to see to the farm stock. The baa-ing and the moo-ing and the sharp voice of the dog soon had her out of bed and downstairs to put the kettle on.

"Bon jour, Madame."

"Bon jour, Monsieur."

"Ça va ?"

"Ça va bien."

She sat on the stone bench by the door with her tea, noting the man's strength and competence as he filled feeding troughs, scattered corn, checked the piglets before releasing them into the steep pasture with their proud mother. She would have to paint him. Paint him at his work. This quietly authoritative man.

"A cup of tea, Monsieur ?" she called, getting up to refill her blue and white bowl.

He followed her into the kitchen. Shyly now. As if trespassing. While she was pouring the tea, he took a basin from the dresser for the three brown eggs he'd brought her still warm and mucky from the hen house, and put it on the table.

"Oh, thank you. Thank you, Monsieur."

They sat outside drinking their tea in comfortable silence. Across the valley a lone bell began to toll urgently.

"Le Dimanche, huh !" Mr Forêt whistled to the dog who was investigating something in the barn, and was gone.

Rosemary sat sunning herself another minute or two, and then went in to gather up her painting gear. The morning was still fresh though the sun was already high as she closed the gate behind her and set off down the lane into the unknown territory beyond the farmstead. Dropping down to what could only be the Vallée Verte, it petered out into a steep grassy track. The hedges were wild with trailing bramble and honeysuckle. And suddenly, there she was on the river bank, a wide sweep of well-grazed turf on this side, birch woods on the other. The river was clear at this point and fast flowing. A family of ducks disturbed by her arrival waddled down for a swim. A perfect picture.

With her collapsible easel and the camping stool set up in the shade of a small stand of silver birch, Rosemary was soon engrossed in her painting. She worked in oils. Boldly and confidently these days, with no more than a few charcoal guidelines.

From somewhere up stream she could hear voices and the intermittent drone of a chain saw. Once or twice as she worked people passed by. A lad on a bike, whistling. A trio of teenage girls dressed for Church. But otherwise she was alone. Apart from the ducks who when they realised she was no threat came and settled down in the long cool grass at her feet.

"I'll bring you some bread tomorrow," she told them in English. "And right now I'll immortalise you on canvas." And she added them to the foreground, a procession of ducks waddling towards her still glistening from their swim."There - what do you think ?" And she stood back from the finished canvas with a glow of intense happiness. Yes, she had managed to capture the sunlight dancing on the water as it tumbled over the weir. Yes.

"You certainly have a way with water," Edward had said, the first time they met. The day she'd finally plucked up the courage to go to his gallery and offer him her work. He'd come out to the car to look over the samples she'd brought along to show him. Between them they'd carried the whole lot inside. He'd given her a cup of coffee while he explained his terms.

"Mm - I like them. I'll hang the lot for you. Let's shift things round a bit, shall we. So that they catch the eye of the punter as he comes in. How about that ? Splendid !"

Blast him ! Rosemary gave herself a shake and looked at her watch. It was getting on for four o'clock. And she was starving.

As soon as she got home she opened the bottle of wine and tore off a hunk of bread which she ate ravenously while she lit the fire and then beat two of the eggs for an omelette.

Later, with the curtains drawn, she dragged the Windsor rocker through from the other room and settled down to listen to the Emperor Concerto that, against all the odds, her portable radio was able to pick up from Paris.

"A Windsor rocker !" Edward would have said. "A Windsor rocker in France ! Come on, Rosie - get your facts straight. Please."

It helped, remembering his faults. Helped a little. With the grief. The desolation. Though it was the other memories that kept breaking through. That funny little laugh of his. The small cries of ecstasy. The delicious smell of him fresh from the bath.

But that was no good. She'd go mad if she started down that path.

The day had helped. The quiet and the solitude. The exhilaration she always felt when she was working. A feeling of more than simple achievement. Almost a sense of spiritual fulfilment. Wonderfully healing and comforting. Edward had already faded a little, become a little shadowy. He was beginning to disintegrate in her head. She would soon be well again.

As the last log burned low she went through to run the bath, and warmed some milk to take up to bed with her.

From now on, this was to be the pattern of Rosemary's days. All much the same. Passing as in a dream, in silence and solitude. A fortnight of this and she should be quite recovered. Strong enough to face Edward and Miranda and the world once more.

Most days there was a trip to the village. To the butcher or the boulangerie.

"Bon jour, Madame. You are enjoying your holiday, alors."

"Today we have strawberry tarts, Madame, the first of the season. You will try one, perhaps ?"

"Today we have some excellent pâté. You will try a little, Madame ?"

She began to do all her shopping at the supermarket. Travellers cheques could be cashed there. She could park easily and wheel her trolley out to the car. Petrol was sold at the EXIT just like at home. But the main attraction of shopping at Bon Marché was its impersonality. There was no need during her transactions to exchange a word with anyone.

It wasn't that she was anti-social exactly. She simply felt she couldn't muster the energy for the cheerful chit-chat of Madame Le Goff in the Bakery, Mr Chirac on the charcuterie stall. She needed silence and solitude. She needed recovery time.

Mr Forêt came and went. Tending the animals. Tinkering with the tractor in the barn. Sometimes she had a word with him. Sometimes she didn't.

"The crop . . . ?" she asked him one morning as she opened the heavy gate to let the tractor through. And spreading her arms wide

34

to indicate the grey-green blanket covering the land in all directions, "what crop is it ?"

"Le tourne-soleil," he told her. "What do you call it, now - sunflower ? Yes. Sunflowers are grown for their oil. It is a very valuable crop. Sunflower seed oil. You understand ?"

She was usually up and about before he arrived to milk his two cream-coloured cows. He kept her provided with milk which he'd leave at the door in a white enamelled can with a hinged lid. There'd be a pot of cream for her sometimes. Eggs, perhaps. A few tomatoes. And every day he brought logs and kindling from the barn and, knocking at the door first, he stacked them along the hearth ready for her evening fire.

He didn't enquire again about her husband, for which she was thankful. While she was not sorry to have someone pottering about the farmyard, it suited Rosemary perfectly that neither of them intruded on the other.

The weather was glorious.

In the dark depths of the wardrobe she had discovered a straw hat, wide-brimmed, fraying and faded, which she borrowed. Now she was able to spend most of the hours of daylight out of doors without fear of sunstroke. Wandering along the river bank. Through the birch woods. Weaving her way through the fields of sunflowers, shoulder high already, their heavy heads still green and tight.

She'd take a length of baguette with her, a hunk of cheese, a plastic tonic water bottle filled with wine. When she grew tired from her rambles, she'd put aside her paint-brush, her crayons, her charcoal, and stretch out luxuriously to sleep in the shade.

Slowly she was healing. After the trauma of Aunt Mary's helplessness and death, after the agony of Edward's defection, Rosemary was coming back to life. And she was working again. Working hard.

By the Friday, she had two unfinished oils, three water-colours and a host of charcoal sketches propped around the sitting room. They were good. She knew they were. Possibly her best work yet.

That evening there was no hot water for her bath. She heated a pan-full on the stove and had a strip wash by the sinking fire. Next morning she kept a lookout for Mr Forêt to tell him about the water heater.

"Ah - it will be the Camping Gas. Maybe it is used up. I have another cylinder in the barn. If I may come through and look at it, please." '

"But of course . . ." And she ushered him in.

In the sitting room he stopped in amazement.

"But, Madame - these are yours ? Your work ? I had no idea you were an artist. They are, they are magnifique !"

When he'd fixed the problem in the bathroom, he lingered on his way out to take a closer look at the pictures.

"Rosemary Richardson, eh ?" he said, deciphering the signature on the largest of the oils. "I like that name. It's good. Rose-Marie. A good name for an artist, si."

"I'll make us some coffee, shall I ?" she said. And left him leafing through the sketch block that happened to be lying on the sofa.

"I'm very interested in art," he told her when she came back with the steaming bowls of café-au-lait, "I've been a teacher most of my life. Well, a lecturer. An Art Historian, in fact. So you see, I do know something about painting."

"But . . . but the farm . . . ?" Rosemary was speechless at this information.

"It's the family farm, as I told you. When my father died a few years back I decided to come home, look after my mother, keep the place going. Fortunately I was able to take early retirement. From college, you understand. And I must admit I'm enjoying the life."

"But why don't you live here in the farmhouse then ? How can you give the place over to heartless holiday makers like me ? If it were mine, nothing would shift me . . ."

"It was my wife," he said. "She'd been used to city life, Yvonne. A modern apartment in Bordeaux. She stuck it out for two or three years, it's true. But she was never happy here. When Mother died, last winter it was, we moved into a flat in town. It was for the best probably. In the truck it's only five minutes away. Ten on the bike."

"Well, I'm happy here, Monsieur . . ."

"Oh, look - please. This is ridiculous. Hugo is my name. Now that we know each other better, perhaps I may call you Rose-Marie ? Oui ?"

That night, wallowing in a good hot bath, Rosemary realised with a pang that her holiday in France was half over. This time next Saturday she would be on her way back across the Channel. On her way home.

36

Chapter Seven

Monday morning it was raining.

Rosemary was still in her dressing gown, coaxing the kindling to life on last night's warm ash, when Mr Forêt tapped at the door.

"Oh - pardonnez-moi, Madame, er, Marie-Rose - there is a letter for you. I met the postman on my way."

"A letter ! But nobody knows where I am."

And then she saw the handwriting. The bold black italic script. Edward's handwriting. Oh, at last ! At last he'd written. He knew the address, of course he did. Hadn't he been the one to write off and book the gîte. Perhaps, oh perhaps . . .

"Thank you. Merci, Monsieur."

And in her eagerness to be alone, alone with her Edward, she practically shoved Hugo Forêt out into the farmyard, out into the downpour, and closed the door firmly on him.

"Edward !" she cried aloud then. "Edward, my love !"

And clutching the pale blue envelope greedily to her flowered cotton wrap she whirled over to the rocker beside the fire, and prayed that the letter brought good news. Regrets, perhaps. Sorrow for the pain he had caused her. Explanations.

"I know it's a lot to ask, but can you forgive me . . . it was only a fleeting fancy . . . it isn't Miranda I want to share my life with . . . it's you, Rosie. It's you."

For a moment Rosemary persuaded herself that this was what Edward had actually written. She studied the handwriting closely as if to detect his message from the envelope. She tried to decipher the postmark, to discover where and when he'd posted it.

But wait a minute - she was going too fast. The letter must be opened with due ceremony. This was undoubtedly a moment of intense significance. Possibly the turning point of her life. Things must be done properly.

She propped the envelope against the jar of wild flowers on the table. The fire had caught and was blazing merrily. Rosemary balanced three good logs on it before running upstairs to dress. Rather than the Indian cottons, the Greek sandals that she'd been floating around in until now, this was a day for jeans and woolly socks and trainers. A day for the soft grey jersey, well-worn and baggy, that Edward liked so much.

"Mm - can't keep my hands off you in that old thing. Come here. Never mind the bloody supper. Come here, woman. Wurgh ! How you get me going, you gorgeous Earth Mother, you ! Lovely ! Lovely ! Oh, no ! **Lovely** !"

Scurrying back downstairs, she put a pan of water on the gas, and ground a measure of beans in Mr Forêt's grandmother's coffee mill. She hummed to herself as she made her preparations. Everything must be just so, she thought, glancing blissfully at the blue envelope propped against the vase of moon-daisies and poppies on the red-and-white oilcloth. Every detail must be treasured up.

She poured herself some coffee, and with the envelope in her hand sat down to read it at last.

Well, in a minute or two. When she'd had a sip of coffee. When she'd savoured the moment to the full.

No painting today, she decided. Not with the rain. And all the excitement. Today she would huddle over the fire. Write up her diary. A letter to Betsy. A few cards to the family. And a letter to Edward, of course. She would forgive him anything. Everything. Miranda was bewitching. No question. With that flaming head of hair. Her childish figure. Her look of innocence, in spite of young Tommy. She could understand Edward falling for the girl. She could understand perfectly.

It might still be possible for him to come over to France and join her. For the few remaining days. In fact she'd ask Mr Forêt - er, **Hugo** - she'd ask him if they could have the place for an extra week. Yes. She'd ask him now.

"Monsieur !" she called, standing at the back door out of the rain. "Er - Hugo !"

"Hello !" He squelched across the yard in gumboots and oilskins, a piglet squirming in his arms.

"Come in. Come in a minute. There's something I want to ask you."

He handed her the piglet while he pulled off his muddy boots and the dripping oilskins.

"The runt," he told her. "I'm afraid it's not going to survive. Not with so much healthy competition. He's the last of fourteen, poor little sod."

"Help yourself to coffee," she said. When she carried it across to the rocking chair, the piglet settled on her lap with small grunts of pleasure.

"Et alors ?" He stood there quietly steaming, his foot on the hearthstone, an arm resting on the mantleshelf.

"Is there any chance of staying on here a little longer ? Another week perhaps ? Have you got other people coming in after me ? When my time's up ? From Saturday ?"

She held her breath. Dear God, please, please . . .

"I told you, you are my first guest. But also my only guest. I have no other bookings so far."

"Then, please, would it be possible for me, for *us* to stay on for a while ? For an extra week, perhaps ? You see, it's my, er, my husband. He's hoping to come over and join me after all. The letter. The letter is from him."

Mr Forêt was looking at her oddly she realised.

"Well ? Can we ? Can we stay on for a bit ?"

Instead of answering, he bent down and picked up the un-opened letter that had somehow slipped to the floor during all the excitement.

"But you have not yet opened the letter . . ."

The piglet squealed, fell off her lap and made a puddle on the floor as she took the letter from him.

"Oh. No. But I feel certain he will be coming. That was the plan, you see. He was to let me know as soon as he could get away. He'll be flying to Poitiers, I expect. I'll drive down and pick him up at the airport."

"Madame, you can stay as long as you like," he told her stiffly, mopping up the puddle with a rag from under the sink before going over to put his waterproof gear on again.

"Oh, bless you !" she cried.

When he'd gone, the piglet snuggled inside the jacket of his oilskins, then at last Rosemary opened the letter, tearing at the stiff blue envelope, frantic suddenly to see what Edward had to say.

"Dear Rosemary," he'd written, **"I know I've treated you very**

**badly, but with such a difference in our ages we always knew
there could be nothing permanent or official between us. At
least let me be the one to give you our good news. I think I owe
you that. Miranda and I are getting married . . ."**

From the pigstye Hugo heard her grief-stricken cry, and came
dashing back to the house.

"Eh bien, Marie-Rose. Now then, now then. Easy now, girl."

An invitation card decorated with cherubs and silver bells
fluttered out of Edward's envelope onto the flagstones.

"Gently now . . ."

She was leaning hopelessly against the mantlepiece, shaken by
sobs. The remains of the letter was blackened and curling to dust
on the fire. Hugo put a hand lightly on her hunched shoulders.

"Doucement, chérie . . ."

She turned to him, burying her distress in his wet and smelly
overalls.

He let her cry. When at last she began to quieten down, he sat
her in the rocking chair, and digging round in the depths of the sideboard, came up with a dusty bottle of cognac.

"Drink this," he ordered, wrapping her numb fingers carefully
around the glass.

He'd kicked his boots off yet again, and she could hear him
upstairs. When he came back with a warm checked rug which he
tucked round her gently, she began to cry all over again.

"Oh, Monsieur - you are being so kind."

"I'll be around the yard all morning," he told her, refilling her
glass, and putting another log on the fire. "Shout if you need me."

And just as he was going out of the door he spotted the radio on
the windowsill and switching it on experimentally, left her with
Schubert.

Sick and hollow, numb, humiliated, Rosemary let the chair rock
quietly in time to the haunting sadness of the String Quintet.
Gradually, with the warmth of the fire, the enveloping comfort of
the plush rug, she drifted into an uneasy sleep.

Edward, oh Edward . . .

And there she was, back in his Gallery, one dismal winter day.

"Darling," he'd cried, as she'd struggled in, her arms full of

40

landscapes, pushing the swing doors open with her bum. "Just what the doctor ordered, this dreary afternoon."

He'd taken the paintings from her, propping them behind the desk, going out with her to collect the last ones from the car.

"These are splendid, Rosie. You get better all the time."

"Oh, go on with you."

"Busy ?"

"Not specially."

"Good."

And he'd gone over and fixed the CLOSED sign on the door, locking it firmly, pulling down the blind. "Come on, my lovely - bed !"

And giggling like kids playing truant, they'd sneaked up the spiral stairs to his flat.

"Oh, Edward . . ."

She must have cried aloud this time. She opened her eyes to find Hugo was there. He'd pulled another chair up to the fire, and he was feeding the piglet from the baby's bottle.

"Ça va ?"

"I'll be all right now. Thank you."

The dog had been asleep too, she saw. Its head on its paws on the hearthstone. Now it jumped up, barking.

"Give it to me," she said, holding out her hands for the suckling piglet as Hugo got up to investigate. And somehow it comforted her, holding the helpless scrap of life that snuffled contentedly on her lap long after the bottle was empty. Rocking together by the fire, with the rain streaming down outside, and Mozart on the radio now.

That evening, needing company for once, and needing to contact Betsy, she drove into the village soon after dark, and again made her way to the Coq d'Or.

"Bon soir, Madame." Anton greeted her warmly. "I thought you had forgotten us."

"Can I use the phone ?" she asked him. "I need to ring home. I'll reverse charges if possible."

He found the International Code she needed, and busied himself tactfully at the far end of the bar. She got through immediately.

"Betsy - hello, love."

"Oh, Ma - hang on, let me turn the telly off. Right. How's it going ? Are you OK ? Have you heard from him ?"

"That's mainly why I'm phoning. I got a letter today." Suddenly she could hardly trust herself to speak.

"What a bloody sod, eh ! You must be shattered."

"No. No, I'm fine. Bit of a shock, but I should have expected it really. I'm all right now."

"They actually asked me to be the bridesmaid, can you believe !"

"You'll be a lovely bridesmaid."

"Fat chance . . ."

"Look, I've decided to stay on. Just for another week or two. I like it here. I'm working hard. There's no particular reason to come back. The farmhouse happens to be available, so I thought . . ."

"Not chickening out are you, Ma ? Not running away ?"

"Not exactly." Though she couldn't deny that today's bombshell had decided it for her. "But the countryside is an inspiration. Sunflowers. Everywhere, in all directions, sunflowers. Wait till you see what I've been doing."

"I should have gone over there with you, Ma. I am a pig. Steve said I shouldn't have let you go on your own like that. Sorry. I'm a pig."

"I love pigs, actually. I've spent most of the day cuddling a piglet . . ."

"Honestly ? That sounds great ! Wish I was with you, but I go back to college tomorrow. Steve's coming down for me in the van."

"I thought I might have missed you. That you'd left already. Make sure you lock everything up and switch everything off, won't you. You could just let Nan know what's happening. Just in case. I'll bring her a bottle or two when I come home."

"I was nattering to her over the wall this morning. She was quite happy to keep an eye on the place till Saturday. She won't mind if it's longer. But are you sure you're OK, Ma ? I'd have been shattered if it was my Steve."

"Bless you, dearie. But there's no need to worry about me. I'm really happy here. I love the farmhouse. I love the solitude. And I'm painting like mad. It would be a pity to come back yet, when I don't have to."

"Well, don't brood, will you. I've seen you before with your love life in ruins. You need someone around to jolly you up."

"It's all right. This evening I've come out for a meal . . ." Rosemary held the phone up so that the chatter at the tables and the clatter Anton made washing glasses behind the bar could be heard in Hampshire. " . . . to cheer myself up. You know."

"Oh, poor old Ma. I do know how much the bugger meant to you. I can just about imagine how I'd feel if my Steve ditched me."

The pips went again.

"Bye then lovey."

"Bye, Ma !"

Rosemary put the phone back, and scuttled through to the smelly loo across the yard. To repair her face. But she couldn't fool Anton.

"Tonight you are my guest, Madame," he insisted, pouring her a glass of wine.

"Mais non . . ."

"Mais oui."

And so it was. She tried the escargots this time, hesitantly, and found them surprisingly good. It was quieter here on a Monday night. Again, Rosemary joined Anton at the big table under the window, though he had to get up and serve every now and again. His young assistant was not on duty tonight.

They were tucking into strawberry tarts when the Fortune Teller came in.

"Eh, bon soir, bon soir . . ." Anton brought glasses and another bottle to the table. "I didn't expect to see you again so soon, mes amis. Permit me to introduce Madame Richardson, a visitor from Angleterre."

"*Rosemary*, please," she said firmly, shaking hands all round. "Rosemary Richardson."

There were three of them. Two young men, and a woman of Rosemary's own age, or maybe older. They all settled round Anton's big table and the Monday night gloom was suddenly alive with laughter and banter.

"Have you got it with you, Lucille ?" somebody called across from another table. "Are we going to have a session ?"

There was a pause while Lucille rummaged fruitlessly in her large handbag.

"Unfortunately . . ."

But it was all part of the ritual apparently. One of her young friends stood up and lifting aside her long un-naturally black ponytail he gently, almost reverently, unclasped the fine silver chain from Lucille's neck, and giving her a ceremonial kiss on the cheek, put it in her hand. Suspended from the chain was a sizeable chunk of pink-ish crystal, rough and unworked. A pendulum.

By this time everyone in the bar had gathered around the big table, bringing their stools and chairs with them.

"Eh, bien - who has a question for the pendulum tonight ?"

And the Fortune Telling began.

* * *

Chapter Eight

By the time she got back to the farm that night, Rosemary had all but recovered from the pain that Edward's letter had given her. Indeed, she was so full of excitement at what she'd witnessed in Anton's bar that she could scarcely wait to get home and find herself something that would serve as a pendulum. Something small but heavy. Preferably something impregnated with her own vibes.

What was there among the bits and pieces she had brought to France with her ?

She didn't really go in for jewellery. She had Billy's beads with her, of course - the long string of small brightly coloured wooden beads that he had threaded for her himself to give to her on Mothering Sunday, his first term at school. And the friendship braid that Betsy had made for her a couple of years back when they were all the rage, in brightest rainbow silks which hadn't faded although she'd worn it ever since, day and night. On her painting wrist. To inspire and protect her, Betsy had said, tying it on firmly.

But neither of these would do.

Having searched her bag, her suitcase, the oddments beside her bed, Rosemary looked around for other possibilities. Aunt Mary's wooden box of skittles was on the windowsill. She took it down, opened the lid, and balancing on the mounting block, tipped the contents out onto the bedspread. The little figures sprawled about, their painted faces so wonderfully individual, watching her intently. There was nothing here that she could use as a pendulum. The sheet of faded flowery wall-paper with which the box was lined had fallen out on the bed with the wooden mannikins. And now she noticed at the bottom of the box, trapped in a joint, was a postcard. A black and white picture postcard. A photograph of a village street. Faded. Non-descript. But unmistakably French.

St Julien le Grand, Perigueux, the caption told her.

She turned it over. It was addressed not to Aunt Mary, as she might have expected, but to Mother.

Mme Betsy Fryer, c/o Orchard Cottage, Isle St Agnes, Somerset, Angleterre. "Remembering always." That was all. The postmark was blurred, but Rosemary made some of it out : Juin 1945.

How mysterious. How intriguing. Was the postcard in the box by chance? Was there a link between the card and the wooden nine-pins? She went downstairs again to look for St Julien le Grand on the map, but got side-tracked. On the kitchen dresser her eye was caught by a heavy carafe with a cut glass stopper. Ah! Here was her pendulum. In the table drawer she found a tangle of string, and tied a piece firmly round the neck of the stopper, leaving a good six inches from which to suspend it. It had none of her vibes on it unfortunately, but perhaps it would work for her all the same.

Dangling the make-shift instrument between thumb and forefinger as Lucille had demonstrated earlier, "Show me my YES," Rosemary instructed it out loud. Slowly at first, but quickly gaining speed and momentum, the glass weight at the end of the string began to swing, rotating smoothly in a clockwise direction. Her YES signal. Amazing!

"Show me my NO."

The pendulum gave a little hiccup and changed to a backwards-and-forwards swing. Backwards-and-forwards, backwards-and-forwards. This was obviously her NO.

Filled with astonishment and excitement, Rosemary sat down at the table to experiment.

"Am I right to stay on here?" she asked.

The glass stopper took a few seconds to respond, but once it got going there was no question about the answer. It swung round-and-round clockwise. Round-and-round. A definite YES.

"Does Edward still love me?" A backwards-and-forwards swing, no two ways about this. NO. "Not a little? Not at all?" NO. NO. NO.

"How am I going to survive without him?" she asked, a sudden wave of desolation washing over her. But this got the pendulum flummoxed. Obviously, like a computer, it could only give a YES or NO answer. It couldn't express an opinion. Try again. Try re-phrasing the question.

"Am I going to survive without him?" Now the answer was clear enough. YES. YES. YES.

With a lighter heart Rosemary ran the bath, and when she was ready, she took the pendulum up to bed with her. There were so many questions she needed to ask.

Chapter Nine

Rosemary sat up very late, experimenting with the pendulum, playing with the little wooden figures laid out on the quilt around her.

Why, this one's rather like Edward, she thought, picking up a skittle that had been carved in the form of a medieval knight, with a sword against his right thigh and a plumed helmet in his left hand, which though carved from wood, really gave the impression of steel and feathers.

The knight's eyes were black under strong brows, with an aggressive glint in them. So like Edward. Why hadn't she noticed before ? Like Edward when he was crossed. When his opinion was challenged, his expertise questioned.

Rosemary packed the other figures away in their box, and took the bold knight into bed with her.

How she knew that look.

"I'm sorry, Rosemary, but I do know what I'm talking about. Your daughter seems to be forgetting that not only am I an expert in the field of Fine Arts but an expert of some standing. I'm afraid that as ever, she is quite mistaken about this. Pissarro is renowned for . . ." Edward's fingers drummed dangerously on the kitchen table.

"Oh, don't give us all that crap again, Mr Bloody Wonderful."

"Betsy !"

"It's no good, Ma. I know you're besotted with him, but personally I'm sick to death of your precious Toy Boy and his fucking pontifications."

"Betsy !"

"He doesn't know everything by a long chalk. He's been wrong a time or two, but I've kept my mouth shut. Our Mr Lucas is a bit of an expert too. He's written books about Art, hasn't he. And he went to Cambridge. He was telling us about Pissarro, Camille Pissarro, today, right. Double Art, last two periods, right. He told us . . ."

Betsy had taken History of Art in the Sixth Form. Along with her Science subjects, Chemistry, Physics and Biology. Art was her 'Fun' subject.

"My dear girl, you and your precious Mr Lucas. Believe me, Charles B Lucas is nobody, but nobody in the Art World. Why do you think he's teaching, for a start ? We all know what they say about teachers. And as far as the Impressionist Movement goes, well . . ."

"Oh, shut up. You and your crappy opinions. You can't talk to me like that. So big. So bloody full of yourself."

"For God's sake girl, what's come over you . . . ?"

"He doesn't belong here with us, Ma. He doesn't live here, even if he is round here all the time. Why doesn't he piss off - **pissarro** bloody off - and find someone else's mother to screw."

"Betsy ! How dare you talk like this ? To Edward ? To anyone ?"

But the angry seventeen year old had stormed up to her room.

"Honestly, Rosemary, she's impossible. Completely impossible. You let her get away with murder. I don't understand why you put up with it. It's so feeble of you. If she was mine, and heaven forbid - well, as a mother you're little short of a disaster. What a performance."

"Oh, come on. She's only a kid. You have to expect a few outbursts at this stage. The divorce has left her vulnerable. She probably sees you as something of a threat."

Helplessly, wondering where she'd gone wrong, Rosemary started to clear the table.

"Finish off the wine, love, while I make some coffee."

"No, I'm sorry. No coffee for me. I have to go. I can't stay after that. Obviously I can't. It really is too bad. Especially as it's *Shogun* in a minute. It's the last episode tonight, in case you'd forgotten. That's mainly why I came round. It really is infuriating."

Edward didn't have a television set himself. This was one of his little vanities, Rosemary suddenly realised, though it hadn't struck her before. People of his sort - cultured, arty, trend-setters - had no time for telly. At least, that was the theory.

"I'll phone Tom," he said, helping himself. "They're sure to be watching. See if I can pop round there."

Fortunately, Edward had cultivated a wide circle of friends with TV sets. He usually managed to see everything he wanted to. Without sacrificing his principles.

Well, he'd be having to change his ideas now with Miranda

48

around. She loved the telly. Sat in front of it for hours, spinning perhaps, or knitting the huge multi-coloured jersies she made a living of sorts from, watching everything indiscriminately - cowboys, the soaps, quiz shows, kids programmes. She'd never survive without the telly.

Suddenly remembering it, Rosemary delved under the bedclothes for the pendulum, and holding it over the little wooden knight sorted out her question. "Has Edward now got TV ?" YES. YES. Serves him bloody right, she thought, not without spite. Pretentious idiot.

There had been other scenes of the same kind, though none quite as nasty so far as she could recall. Betsy knew she'd behaved abominably and to make amends did her best to avoid confrontations.

"Look, Betsy, love, aren't you being a wee bit childish about Edward ? *I want my Mummy all to myself.* That kind of thing."

It was the night after this terrible outburst. Betsy had brought Ovaltine up for them, Rosemary remembered. She was sitting cross-legged on the bottom of her mother's bed in the old green dressing-gown they'd got her for the Outward Bound holiday in the Third Form. They'd have to buy her a new one for college. The kid looked so terribly young and vulnerable with her thin wrists sticking out of the skimpy sleeves.

"Give me some credit, Ma. I'm not into all that Oedipus stuff. You know I'm not. I've been quite civilised with your other boyfriends, haven't I ? It's just that . . ."

"I know. I know what the problem is. It's his age, his youth that bugs you. I should never have allowed myself to get involved with him, considering . . ."

"No, it's not that. I wouldn't care if he was *my age*, for Christ's sake, if I thought he was making you happy. It's something about him. I can't explain. His arrogance. His public school manner. I can't understand what you see in him. Quite frankly, he's an arrogant sod. And a phoney."

"Don't say that, please. I know you rub each other up the wrong way, but he can be really sweet."

"Oh, yeh ! You could have fooled me !"

It was easier once she started college and Steve came into the picture. She was hardly ever home, for a start. But it didn't mean her feelings had changed.

"Steve reckons . . ."

"Yes ? What does Steve reckon ?"

"He reckons he's using you, your Edward. Till someone more suitable comes along. Look how often he turns up for supper, say, your Toy Boy. And then bumbles off as soon as you've fed him, to meet his trendy friends. His Arty-Crafty contacts. He doesn't invite you along, does he . . . ?"

"He does sometimes. It's the arrangement we have. Not to monopolise one another. I don't always want to be trailing around with him. It suits me, the way we are."

"Oh, yeh ! I'm not stupid, Ma ! I know what he's doing to you. He's round here when it suits him. Otherwise . . ."

"It's not true. We each need our space."

"Steve has got him weighed up, don't worry. Steve can't stand him any more than I can."

"Well, I'm not too fond of Steve, if we're being honest."

"You hardly know him. You haven't given him a chance."

"I do know Edward. And I like him. I love him, if you must know."

"Love him ! You don't love him, Ma. You bloody adore him, that's your problem."

Oh, Christ ! The bitter truth ! Now she came to face up to it, it was perfectly true. The enslavement of love.

Edward had got into the habit of coming to eat with them three or four nights a week. Never invited her back to eat at his place, not once the initial excitement had gone out of it. Never suggested they went out for a meal either.

She remembered a recent incident that she'd avoided analysing. Till now.

"Rosie - hi ! I've got to drive over to Monks Barton later this morning. To pick up a couple of pictures. Thought we could have a pint on the way, if you're free. How about it ?"

Great ! There were so few outings nowadays.

Sitting on the terrace of the Brown Trout with beer and sandwiches, he came out with it.

"Guess this evens up the score, Rosie. Salves the old conscience somewhat. And sweetens you up for a few more of those excellent casseroles of yours, eh !"

With horror she now forced herself to listen to her inane reply.

50

"You've no need to feel like that, love. I'm cooking anyway, for Betsy, Miranda, young Tommy, and Steve as often as not. There's nothing gives me more pleasure than seeing you tuck into a good square meal with us. Well, scarcely anything."

"As far as that goes, I'll have to drop you off in the town when we get back. I'm tied up this afternoon. And will have to dash off straight after supper again tonight. Sorry about that. There's an Awareness Raising session out at Jack's place. I've promised to lead the meditation."

Rosemary glowered at the little wooden figure on the quilt. My God, she had been well and truly besotted.

He borrowed her car whenever his own was out of action. Taking it for granted that she would manage without it. But it was a different matter the odd time she found herself without transport.

"I'm sorry, Rosie, but my business must come first. I've never lent my car to anyone. That's just the way I feel. I'm surprised you asked me, actually."

She'd put his friends up over night a time or two. His parents. Even an ex-girlfriend. And gladly.

But, come on, now - let's be honest, she told herself grimly. If ever I needed something . . .

"Look, Rosie, let's not start leaning on one another. OK. You solve your problems. I solve mine. As the Lord Buddha said, all our pain comes from our attachments. Let's avoid commitments, please, And expectations. Just take what's offered without analysing it. Without weighing it up. OK ?"

He couldn't half waffle, she realised, once he got going. And in his Buddhist phase he waffled worst of all.

Why do I get myself into these bloody things, Rosemary wondered. I'm not a complete idiot, so why do I go along with it ?

And, while she was looking at things so straight, there was her birthday, wasn't there. That was an eye-opener, according to Betsy.

"Happy birthday, Mumsie-Wumsie. And for Christ's sake, open it carefully."

Last year, it had fallen on a Sunday. Tactfully leaving them to themselves for the birthday weekend, Betsy had gone over to stay with her father. It was pretty late when she got back home on the birthday night.

"Oh, Betsy, it's beautiful. Simply beautiful. But what is it? Whatever is it?"

"It's a witchball. To keep witches away. And evil. And the forces of darkness. Do you like it? No need to pretend. I'm old enough to handle a major disappointment."

"Don't be so daft. It's absolutely gorgeous. Where did you find such a thing?"

It was a delicate silver ball, like a Christmas tree bauble, but bigger than a grapefruit.

"In the Antique Market. I've had my eye on it for weeks. Been negotiating with that funny old girl, you know the one, on the junk stall in the corner. She only let me have it after I'd pointed you out to her. Coming out of Sainsbury's, you were, one day last week. It's bad luck, bad magic, to buy a witchball for yourself, you see. If you're meant to have one, it will come to you. As a gift. Isn't that divine, eh? She had to vet you before she'd sell me the thing. And even then she wouldn't take money for it - I'm to look after her stall for a couple of Saturdays for her. Quite divine, don't you agree?"

They hung it up there and then. In the window of Rosemary's studio which happened to look out onto the front path.

"Great! That's perfect for it. It has to hang where it can scrutinise everyone who comes to the door. Witches can't abide them. If she should catch sight of her own reflection in one of these, a witch will shrivel up and vanish. It's true, Ma. No need to look like that."

They stood staring at the silvered sphere in wonder and delight. The studio light was off, the curtains open, so that it caught the street lights and threw them back outside again.

"Magic," Rosemary said. "Pure magic. You are a love."

"What did Lover Boy bring you, then?" Betsy asked.

"Don't call him that."

"Well . . . ?"

"Well, a box of chocolates, actually."

"A box of chocolates!"

"A very special box. Belgian. From M&S. You know the sort. Frightfully expensive."

"Oh, honestly, Ma - chocolates! I always said the guy was lacking in imagination. Chocolates! Just shows how little thought he put into it. Steve says you can tell how much anybody cares for you, you know, by the presents they give you. If they've used their imagination. If they've noticed, really noticed, the kind of person you are, the kind of things that will bring you pleasure. Fat lot of trouble Mr Wonderful went to. It just bloody goes to show. Chocolates !"

"Come on, now. No need to go mad. Men are never very good at presents, are they."

"My Steve is. He's ace with presents. Look at the ammonite he brought me back from his Field Trip. Look at the postcards he's found me. Wonderful. And that copy of Tennyson. In that incredible second-hand shop in Salisbury. All worn and yellowing with age. Amazing ! He's really good at presents, my Steve is."

"OK - so Edward isn't that imaginative . . ."

Though there had been the watch - his Grandmother's he'd said, but that was early on before the magic began to wear thin.

"Mother ! Wake yourself up, can't you. Edward is a dead loss. You deserve someone special. Yes you do. Never mind this immature jumped-up phoney. Come on, you know I'm right."

"Oh, shut up, can't you ! Have a chocolate, for God's sake. And shut up about it."

"Bloody hell ! You've been wolfing these down, haven't you ? You must have been stuffing yourselves with chocolate all day."

"He's mad on chocolate, isn't he. Specially Belgian ones."

"Oh - so that's it then. No wonder he gave you chocolates, Ma. I *see* !"

Rosemary saw too. At last. How blind she'd been. Dazzled by his youth, his charm. And, yes, by his very arrogance.

"I guess I've had a lucky escape," she said to the little wooden knight, plonking him back in the box with his fellows. "Miranda is welcome to you, young man."

Now she'd have to pop down to the bathroom.

Going through to the kitchen for a drink of milk, Rosemary opened the back door a moment. The rain had stopped at last. It was a still star-lit night. Inspite of the farmyard smells (which she no longer noticed much), the air was fresh and clean. She took a good deep breath. And then another.

That's better, she thought wryly. I'm cured of him. At last.

And, back in bed, she realised how true this was. She had

recovered from Edward as if from a long and debilitating illness. In the morning she'd get back to work. Back into the productive pattern of the last few days. But this time, with no end in sight. Hugo Forêt, bless him, had said she could stay as long as she liked.

Rosemary had all the time in the world in which to paint the fields of sunflowers.

* * *

Chapter Ten

After the downpour, the weather set fair. Day after day, week after week, the sun shone in a cloudless sky. Across the countryside, the sunflowers lifted their heavy heads to follow its flight-path.

Rosemary was usually out with paintbox and easel before the dew had dried on the grass.

"Bon jour, Hugo." His name came naturally to her now.

"Tomorrow I'm taking the lambs to market," he said one morning. "Will you come with me, Marie-Rose ?"

They set off in the old red truck before it was light, with the lambs complaining pitifully in the back, at this their first and last ride.

"Poor little devils," she said. "I don't know how you can do it."

"They have a good life while it lasts. The end is quick and efficient. Like us, they think they're on a charabanc outing. A farmer can't afford to be sentimental."

While he saw to the documentation and all, she found a perch from which she could watch the dealing, and took out her sketch block and pencil.

"Eh bien - you've really captured it," he said, coming back to tell her the lambs had fetched a good price. "We deserve a drink, both of us."

He took her to the Chevalier Noir across the street.

"Ah - Monsieur !" the bar man said, recognising him. "The usual ? And for the lady ?"

She felt very comfortable with him, this large quiet man, who made no demands on her, posed no threat. They sat out on the pavement with their Pernod, enjoying the bustle around them, the buying and selling, the loading and unloading of cattle trucks, the squeals of protest, the urgent mumbo-jumbo of the auctioneer. Somehow, even the strong market smells seemed not offensive but exotic this morning.

"I've one or two things to see to," he said as she drained her glass. "What if we meet here for lunch in let's say an hour ?"

She had things to do as well. Things to buy. Paint, paper, size, and a couple more fine brushes. She certainly didn't want to run out of materials now that the work was going so splendidly.

"An Art Shop - let me think now," and he directed her towards the Square.

It was a fair sized town with wide tree-lined boulevards and bustling side streets. The Square was quite impressive, with stone balustrades on three sides, and shaded by lime trees dripping with sweetness. There were several games of boules in progress. What an odd assortment of men, she thought. Some in jeans and black berets, some in business suits. Young lads, grandfathers, men in their prime. But all apparently equal and equally absorbed in their sacred game.

Next to the Art Shop was a dusty kiosk selling braid and buttons, buckles and beads. For a couple of francs Rosemary found a heavy glass marble with a wire hook through it.

"Off a chandelier, I'd guess," the woman told her, wrapping it carefully in tissue paper. "Genuine crystal."

It would make the perfect pendulum.

That night she got Aunt Mary's box of wooden mannikins down again, and spread the little figures out around her on the bed.

Edward, the angry knight, she quickly dispensed with, shoving him back into the tissue paper and firmly closing the lid of the box on him.

Again, she marvelled at the intricacy of the carving, the brilliance of the colours, the individuality of the characters of the eight carved skittles that were left.

But what was this ? How odd ! How incredible ! Here was the figure of an older man. The King, she guessed. How come she hadn't noticed him before ! He looked quite the intellectual, with his long distinguished face, sharp eyes under bushy brows, a neat beard. Rosie knew this character. She knew him all right.

Putting the other figures safely back in their box beside Edward, she snuggled down into bed with the King.

"Stay behind a moment, please, Miss Fryer," Fred Sixsmith, the Senior Design Lecturer, had said to her early into her second term at college.

"Watch him !" a couple of the girls had warned her under their breath, as they streamed out of the top floor studio making for the

Common Room, coffee and doughnuts. "Fred's got quite a reputation !"

But she hardly heard them. Oh, lord, she remembered thinking. Maybe I'm not making the grade.

"Ah, yes - Miss Fryer. Rosemary. I've been meaning to have a word with you. I'm interested in your work. In my opinion you show considerable promise. I was wondering whether you'd like to come along to a small group that I'm starting ? On Thursday evenings. Tomorrow. In my study."

What a mug she'd been.

"Don't broadcast it around. It could be interpreted as favouritism."

My stars - fancy falling for his patter so easily.

Predictably, no-one else had shown up at the Thursday night gathering. No-one else had been invited. After a perfunctory chat about her efforts in class, he'd produced gin and tonic, ice and lemon. They'd settled down on his studio couch (would you believe !) to discuss her prospects, and that was that.

"My dear child, I can't tell you what this means to me," he'd sighed as she scrambled back into her jeans. "I've had my eye on you for weeks. Couldn't seem to keep you out of my mind. Wondering whether I'd ever get you up here on your own. Mm - you sweet little innocent !"

She clearly wasn't such an innocent, of course. Not after Father. But it was months before she even hinted at those childhood traumas. When she finally found the courage to confide in him, he'd insisted on hearing all the gruesome details.

"But how old were you the first time he actually, you know, actually . . ."

It had definitely excited him.

"The man must have been a fiend. A monster. I can hardly believe it. Do you mean to say he . . ."

Fred Sixsmith had gone at her like an old billy goat that night. Funny, but now she came to think about it, he was old enough to be her father. Easily.

He was incredibly distinguished, Fred. And - oh boy - didn't he know it ! Well over six foot tall. Gangly. With those Denis Healey eyebrows and a mane of dark wavy hair already greying at the temples but none the worse for that. And the beard. She'd certainly never seen such a specimen. Silver with a black stripe running down from his lip. Badger she'd called him. Badger.

57

The small wooden figure in her hand bore a strong resemblance to Badger. And - was it possible - his beard was striped in the same way, silver and black.

"You will be my inspiration," he'd told her that first night. "Like Dante and Beatrice. 'Oh glorious lady of my heart.' Just a sec - I'll check the coast's clear. Don't want to start the tongues wagging, do we. How about Monday night ?"

Poor Fred. He'd had his reputation to consider. His status on the staff. His wife and kids.

Rosemary had seen the sense, of course, in keeping their relationship secret. This was the Sixties. The early Sixties before anyone had started to swing. A strict code of conduct still applied. On their College Campus, anyway. Staff-student affairs were definitely taboo. People still talked of the scandal that had blown up a couple of years earlier when one of the most talented Sculpture students was sent down in disgrace.

It had given Rosemary a delicious sense of romance and intrigue, her affair with Fred Sixsmith. She loved all the cloak and dagger stuff, the stolen moments spiced with the threat of discovery. The cryptic messages.

"Um, Miss Fryer ! Mr Sixsmith asked me to tell you tonight's meeting has had to be cancelled."

Oh, no - St Valentine's Day ruined !

"Come on, Rosie - get a move on ! We're all waiting for you. We'll miss the kick-off if we don't go now. *Come on !*"

"I'm not coming. I haven't got time. This essay has to be handed in on Monday. I'm going to work in the library this afternoon. Sorry."

"Oh, for Christ's sake ! It's Saturday ! It's the Big Match ! Everyone's going to be there cheering the lads on. Never mind the bloody essay. You've all tomorrow for that."

"I hope you appreciate just what I'm sacrificing for you, Mr Sixsmith, Sir," she'd told him as he poured their preliminary gins and tonics, secure in the knowledge that the whole damn college would be down on the Field. No fear of interruption.

"Well, I only hope I am able to provide you with as much excitement as our noble Vampires might have done, my girl !"

I wonder if everybody knew what we were up to on his studio couch, Rosemary thought now, stroking the little wooden figure tenderly.

Maybe it was common knowledge all along. Maybe I was too absorbed to realise.

"Have you seen this week's Journal?" he'd asked her as Finals approached. "The 'Sure Sell' people are looking for Arts graduates. As advertising agencies go, it has a good reputation. For recognising potential. I'll write you a reference. Purely professional, of course. I think you should go for it."

"But..."

But it would mean moving to London. It would mean The End. She'd hoped, well she'd half hoped...

Even then, towards the end of her third year, before she'd graduated, before she'd found a job, while she was still in College, she knew he'd started something up with a tiny dark-eyed First Year. That bloody Melissa.

"Sorry, Rosie, but can't make it tonight," he'd said. "Domestic duties, I'm afraid. I'll be in touch."

Domestic duties indeed! Did he think she was simple or something? She'd caught them together a time or two. In the foyer one lunch time. Having an animated but clearly intimate discussion on the main stairs one evening.

"My dear child," Rosemary heard him sigh, "I can't tell you what this means to me..."

She knew his tactics. She knew his taste in students. She knew his persuasive tongue.

God, I'm a fool, she thought again. Such a bloody fool. I always fall for the same kind of bastard. When am I ever going to learn!

But to that question, in spite of his distinguished and intellectual appearance, the little mannikin on the pillow beside her had no answer.

And testing out the splendid new pendulum, she found that unless she could focus her question more accurately, that was no help either.

* * *

59

Chapter Eleven

Arriving back at the farm next afternoon, tired and sticky and flecked with paint after a really productive day beside the river, Rosemary was surprised to see a sleek car at the gate, and sitting in the shade of the mulberry tree beside the barn the familiar curly-haired figure of Anton, chef and patron of Le Coq d'Or. What on earth was he doing in her yard ?

"Bon jour, Madame. Er, Rosemary."

"Monsieur ! This is a surprise. Are you waiting for Hugo, perhaps ?"

"No, no - it's you I want to talk to. I have a proposition to put to you."

"Excuse me a moment then. I must take my things indoors. Can I get you a drink ? I've got into the habit of having a glass of Anis at this time of day."

They sat side by side on the stone bench with their tall glasses.

"Is it OK ? I mix it with a drop of lemonade. To make it go further. It's such a treat."

"Hugo Forêt was in the bar last night and he mentioned your work. In fact he fairly raved about it. It occurred to me that we might be able to help one another."

His idea was that they should exhibit some of Rosemary's work in Le Coq d'Or.

"We get a good many tourists through the town as the summer goes on. I think you might sell a steady number of pictures. And word will get around, and that will boost business for us both. What do you say ?"

"But, but you haven't even seen the kind of thing I do," she said in astonishment. "Better come in and take a look."

By now the farmhouse sittingroom had become an art gallery. An art warehouse. There were paintings everywhere. Stacked against the walls, hanging from the railings of the minstrel's gallery, piled on the uncomfortable sofa. Propped around the wooden pillars. Unframed, of course. Unmounted.

"Mon dieu - you have been busy !" he said, amazed. "They are splendid. Splendid. Hugo is right. You have captured the spirit of our landscape - the light, the sunflower fields, the wide horizons. The spirit of the Charente. You are indeed an artist, ma chère. I shall be proud to display your work around the bar."

While she refilled their glasses, they discussed how many of the pictures he would take initially, what price she should put on them. Having loaded a dozen or so into the boot of his car, Anton suddenly grabbed her and lifting her off her feet swung her round so that her soft Indian skirt whirled out around them.

"We are going to be good for each other, chérie. You will come for supper tonight, yes. As my guest. Before we eat you can help me decide what to hang where - OK ?" And sticking his head out as the car pulled away, he yelled back to her, "No more diluted Anis for you, my friend." And with a pretty convincing American twang, "We will knock it back neat from now on, you and me."

Two of the paintings were sold that very first evening. And much interest was shown in Rosemary's work.

"I am so grateful to you both," Rosemary said, over the Cognac she was treating them to. Hugo had turned up to help hang the pictures, and they'd all eaten together, drinking to their combined success. "This means I can stay on indefinitely. That is, for as long as you are prepared to rent me the farmhouse, Hugo. Without worry. Drink up. Let's have another. And pour one for yourself, Pierre."

The young man behind the bar, his garish tattoos hidden under a jersey tonight, brought over the bottle of Cognac, but refused the drink she offered him. When he took the notes from her he counted out the change almost insolently, she thought. Why was he behaving with such hostility ?

"Excuse me a minute, mes amis . . ." and Anton going to the door as if to attend to those customers who were sitting out at the tables in the lamp-lit Square, beckoned to his young assistant to follow him.

"Pauvre petit Pierre," Hugo said with mock concern. "You have made him jealous."

Jealous ! Oh, that was it, was it ? The charming Anton and this uncouth lad. Well, Pierre had no cause to worry on her account. The last thing she wanted was another relationship. Certainly not one as complicated as that. Not after poor Billy, thank you. No fear of that.

"I'd best be off before I cause more trouble then," she said to Hugo. "Good night !"

And off she went, calling to the two men still arguing intensely at one of their own outdoor tables. "Bon nuit, mes amis, and thank you."

Earlier she had threaded the crystal marble that she'd found at Niort onto a length of fine string, and as expected, it made a beautiful pendulum. Heavy enough to give a good strong swing. Round-and-round for YES. Backwards-and-forwards for NO.

On the carved head-board of the bed Rosemary had discovered an ancient rusty iron hook. A hook from which a lamp might once have been suspended. Or an elaborate tassled cord perhaps, a bell-pull or some such. From this she had hung her new pendulum. Nice and handy for late night interrogations.

Snuggled up now among the plump pillows and the crisp clean quilt, she took down the pendulum.

"Anton," she told the pendulum, and when it had as-it-were tuned in to him, she put the question. "Does he fancy me ?"

The pendulum went into a sort of hiccup, as if not quite sure how to respond and finally settled into a criss-cross swing. Was this a DON'T KNOW signal ? Or PLEASE RE-PHRASE THE QUESTION ?

Try again. "Is he gay ?"

YES. YES. YES.

"Are he and Pierre lovers ?"

YES. YES. YES.

God, how slow she was in the uptake. How come she never cottoned on to these things . . .

He'd been such a beautiful lad, her Billy. With hair as fine and fair as an angel, and wavy with it.

"Should have been a girl, your Billy," she remembered Maggie saying once when they'd shared a holiday all of them. Maggie and Ken and their three lads. Rosemary and Pete, seven year old Billy, and Betsy still in nappies. The time they all had a week on the Isle of Wight. All of them together. Aunt Mary's treat, she remembered now.

"I've a mind to give you a break, Rosie. You're looking right peaky. A week by the sea is what you're needing. No - I know you can't afford it. But my friend Alice that lives in Ventnor, you've heard me talk about her, well she's got a couple of holiday cottages that she lets out and I happen to know one of them is free over Easter. Now, what I'd like to do is treat you to the week. Fares and everything. And I'll settle up with Alice. How do you feel about that ?"

"Pack in as many as you like," Alice had told Aunt Mary. "There's heaps of room."

And there was. The cottage had turned out to be a substantial house that Alice was planning to divide into two flats, each of which would easily sleep six. Until that happened it was all one. A bit tatty perhaps. With nothing more than basic equipment. But it was within a stone's throw of the beach with sea views from the upstairs windows.

"I'm suggesting that Maggie shares the place with you, Rosie," Aunt Mary had phoned to tell her.

"But . . ." Rosemary had never liked her next oldest sister. There'd always been friction between them. Right from the start.

"I know how you feel about her," Aunt Mary seemed to be reading her mind over the phone. "But you are sisters. It's time you buried all that antagonism. You might find you quite like one another now you're grown-up. Give it a chance, will you, my lovely ?"

Pete hadn't been very keen at first. He'd never liked any of Rosemary's family. He thought Maggie was empty headed. That Ken was a snob. But to everybody's surprise it had worked out fine.

"It was the first time we'd ever really talked, Maggie and I," she remembered telling Aunt Mary afterwards. "She was always so horrid to me when we were kids. But I think perhaps we understand each other a bit better now. All the anger's gone out of her since Father died."

"Well, I'm glad about that," Aunt Mary had said. "Sisters should be friends. Look at me and your mother. And neither of you girls has had it easy."

"Look at him ! He should have been a girl, your Billy," Maggie had said one afternoon on the beach.

Her boys were playing football with the two dads. Betsy had been asleep on a towel under a sunshade. But Billy - Billy had been creating a masterpiece in the damp sand. Tracing out delicate patterns of swirls and flowers with a stick. Highlighting the design with carefully selected shells and pebbles. A real work of art.

"Go and play with the others, Billy," she'd said, not wanting him to listen in on their grown-up conversation. Their memories of Life with Father.

"Yes, come on, son," called the paunchy man in the ludicrously bright holiday shirt and toning shorts.

"Do I have to, Mummy ? I want to finish this."

"Go on with you, love. It will soon be tea time. Go on now . . ."

"Are you coming or do I have to fetch you ? We don't want a namby-pamby in the family !" And the football came flying over landing right in the middle of Billy's picture.

"Oh, no - it's ruined ! He's ruined it." And biting back the tears, Billy ran off to hide in the dunes.

"Oh, I'm so sorry," said Pete. "Didn't know I was such a good shot. What a shame."

During that week in Ventnor, Ken and Pete went off to the pub every evening, leaving the sisters to bath the kids and see to the washing and the washing-up and all. The men were never back before closing time.

"I don't know how you put up with Pete," Maggie said towards the end of the week. "How on earth did you come to marry him ? He's more of a chauvinist than my Ken, and that's saying something."

Rosemary could scarcely remember what she'd seen in Pete.

He'd been on the staff of Merrywood High School, where she herself had found a job after college.

"If only I'd been offered that post with the advertising agency," she'd said to Maggie, surprised to hear out loud the thoughts she had bottled up for so long, "I might have become a real artist. And it certainly wouldn't have been Pete I married."

"Yes, but why Pete ?" Maggie had persisted, accepting without comment the verdict on her little sister's marriage.

They'd both been lonely, hadn't they, she and Pete, in their separate dismal digs. Both hating London. Both hating teaching. She'd been missing Fred Sixsmith. Pete had been missing his mother.

"We kind of drifted into it," Rosemary explained lamely. There was never much magic. It had just seemed inevitable. "We started sleeping together, and that was it, somehow. That's how it was in those days. Must have been much the same with you and Ken, wasn't it ? We were all such innocents."

"In spite of Father ?

Rosemary had been taken aback. Had Maggie known, then ? And suddenly with a flash of intuition she realised *how* Maggie knew what Father had done to her. *Why* she knew.

"You too ?" Rosemary asked her older sister. That was all : You too ?

For the first time in their lives the sisters looked straight at one another. Eye to eye.

"All of us. All four of us. One after the other. Didn't you know ? Honestly ? Didn't you guess ?"

Know ? How could she have known. The other girls were so much older than Rosie, for one thing. There were eight, nine years between her and Maggie. By the time she came along, Frances and Kate were already lofty teenagers. Their sufferings were over before Rosie's began.

In any case, all through her childhood she'd been locked in her own private hell. A mixture of disgust, guilt and loathing. And yet with that shameful tingle. Her shameful addiction to Father's vile attentions. Always she'd been alert to his whereabouts in the house. To his mood. His intentions. These factors had dominated Rosemary's childhood. There was no time, no energy left over. No thought for the sufferings of siblings.

"If you knew, if Frankie and Kate knew, why didn't one of us put a stop to it ? Why didn't Mother come to our rescue ?"

"I've no idea. None of us understood Mother. I tried to talk to her about it once. After he was dead. After I was grown up and married. But it was no good. I couldn't get through to her."

"You always had such a wild imagination, Maggie," Mother had said. "Put the kettle on, there's a dear. We mustn't speak ill of the dead."

"Mother must have known, surely. I'd know if Pete was up to something with our kids. Anybody would know."

"She must have known, yes. She must have been afraid of him. Afraid of getting the skeleton out of the cupboard."

"And you knew, Maggie. And yet you were so horrid to me. I was terrified of you, and your vicious outbursts. And all the time you knew what was going on."

"Don't ask me to explain. I can only say that in spite of everything, when Father started messing about with you, I couldn't stand it. I hate to admit it, but I can remember feeling, well - rejected. Cast aside and rejected by the bloody man. I suppose I was jealous of you, his four year old favourite. The latest of his little princesses."

Both sisters were silent at these words, remembering.

"Don't forget, I'd been the favourite until you came along. Much as I hated his goings-on, it really put my nose out of joint when he switched his activities to you."

When they came rolling in from the King's Head at midnight, Pete and Ken seemed surprised to find their wives sitting on the rug beside the gas fire in their dressing gowns, deep in conversation over mugs of Ovaltine.

"I thought you and Maggie had never hit it off," Pete said getting ready for bed.

"We had a real good chin-wag. Cleared up one or two family mysteries."

"Hope you weren't tearing us to bits, me and Ken. I know how you women go on when you're by yourselves."

"We'd more interesting things to talk about, I can promise you."

"Come on, then," he'd said, switching the light off with one hand, and yanking her nightie up around her bottom with the other. "Let's be having you. This sea air makes me horny. Yes. Yes. YES !" And he rolled off her with a grunt.

Thinking of it now so many years later, the best part of twenty years later, Rosemary froze, and a wave of silent protest swept over her.

Father. Pete. No, no, no !

It was ages since she'd had that chin-wag with Maggie. And so much had happened in the meantime. Both of them were now divorced, for one thing. Maggie out in New Zealand with husband number three.

Rosemary wondered whether Aunt Mary had deliberately engineered the Ventnor situation. To force the two girls to confide in each other. She wouldn't put it past their Aunt, bless her !

"Aunt Mary !" she said out loud, not knowing whether the pendulum could tune in to the dead. It took a minute or two to react, and then began to rotate slowly, waiting for the question.

66

"Did Aunt Mary intend us to confide in one another on the Isle of Wight holiday ?" she asked the heavy crystal bead.

YES. YES. No question about that. YES. She'd planned the whole thing with that in mind.

"You interfering old bat," Rosemary said out loud, but laughing.

Then another thought struck her. If Aunt Mary had intended them to speak of their childhood abuse, then obviously she was well aware of what had gone on. Of Father's taste for little girls. The younger the better.

Mother might have been too frightened of her husband to do anything to stop him. But Aunt Mary was frightened of no-one. And with her crusading spirit, how could she stand by knowing the abuse that was going on in her sister's house ?

"Why didn't Aunt Mary do something to protect us ?" Rosemary asked the pendulum.

But of course it could only cope with YES or NO answers. And until Rosemary was a lot nearer the truth there was no help here.

"I must write and ask Frances," Rosemary thought sleepily. "As the oldest, perhaps she knows why Mother turned a blind eye to our sufferings. Yes, I'll write to Frankie in the morning."

And with that settled, she fell asleep, the pendulum clutched tight in her hand.

* * *

Chapter Twelve

Rosemary did try to write to her sister Frances. But it wasn't easy. There was the generation gap, for one thing, with thirteen years between them. They'd never been close, and since Rosemary's divorce they had virtually lost touch.

No, that wasn't quite true. They had exchanged a brief word at Aunt Mary's funeral.

"Quite unsuitable, this," Frances had exclaimed indignantly when she realised that the funeral party was indeed going to walk through Atyeo's Orchard to the Church. "One of your ridiculous ideas, I suppose, Rosemary."

And afterwards when the assembled family learnt that Aunt Mary had left everything, the cottage and everything, to her, Frances had scarcely been able to contain herself.

"Most unfair. Most unjust. Haven't we all done quite as much as Rosemary for the old girl. I never did understand why she was singled out. Aunt Mary knew how I'd set my heart on the rosewood firescreen. And to think we drove all this way . . ."

"You can have the bloody firescreen," Rosemary had interrupted. "Have whatever you like. But go, for God's sake. Just bloody go, and take your pompous husband with you."

No, Rosemary couldn't possibly write and ask Frances about Father. Or why Mother had chosen to turn a blind eye to what was going on.

Rather later than usual this morning, Rosemary set off with paints and easel. The sunflowers were as tall as she was by now, wide open to the sun. The air was heavy with their slightly pungent smell. For once she had no heart for her work. Without even unpacking her things, she found a shady spot beside the river and kicking off her sandals, stretched out on the grass.

It was Rosemary's divorce that had finished Frances.

"I'm thankful Mother did not live to see this," she had written to Rosemary at the time. "Marriage is not supposed to be easy. You have to work at it. But you were never prepared to work at anything, so far as I remember. Most of us stick it out, muddle through, but not Mother's blue-eyed darling. Oh, no. It's Pete and the children we feel sorry for, John and I. Especially Pete . . ."

If only she knew what I'd had to put up with all those years, Rosemary thought. Poor Pete, indeed !

It had been OK at first. While they'd both been teaching. Both earning. Equal. In fact before she fell pregnant with Billy, as Head of Art she'd been earning rather more than he was. Maybe that's what persuaded him the time had come to start a family. It had been a blow to his pride when she was elevated over the heads of three older and more experienced teachers. But at least it hadn't been in his own department, Maths. That would have been an unbearable humiliation for him.

Until the baby was born they had bumbled along in the same joyless fashion as most of their friends and colleagues. It was after Billy arrived that things began to go wrong.

"He doesn't beat me or anything," Rosemary had tried to explain to Aunt Mary once when she'd escaped for a few days to Isle St Agnes with the children in tow. "He doesn't chase after other women. I wish he did, to be honest. Then maybe he'd leave me alone."

Somehow the pattern had become established. Night meant bed. Bed meant sex.

"Why else would a fellow walk up the aisle ?" he'd asked in genuine surprise, when she started her futile protests.

"But it's not love, Pete. It's not even lust. You're simply using my body for your solitary gratification. Might as well use a blow-up doll. It's obscene. Totally obscene."

"Sorry, Rosie. If I don't have it, I simply can't sleep. You should know that by now. But if you feel so strongly about it, fair enough, I'll just read for a bit. See if you change your mind."

When she could, she resisted him, knowing full well he would keep the light on all night if necessary. Until he got his way. If he couldn't sleep he made certain she didn't either, pawing her, touching her. Keeping up a flow of dirty talk which was supposed to turn her on, excite her.

Gradually, worn out and demoralised, she began to submit to his demands.

The ritual was as loveless and predictable as having a pee. And Rosemary usually felt like a piss-pot as she lay there, lifeless, while he discharged into her.

She'd wept many a time, even as Pete pumped away on top of her.

She'd wept again, once the children were tucked up in the attic of Orchard Cottage, and she sat by the fire trying to explain to Aunt Mary how things were at home.

"I don't hate him exactly. I don't think I've ever loved him enough to hate him now. I hate what he does to me night after night. So cold, it is - he's masturbating in me, that's what."

That time, she'd gone back to him of course, but feeling a little stronger for having unburdened herself to Aunt Mary.

"It's not for me to tell you what to do," Aunt Mary had said as they piled back into the car to drive home. "But why don't you get your paints out again. Give yourself an hour or so a day. You should be able to manage that now that Betsy's at school. It won't solve anything, but it might just help. Bye darlings - Billy, Betsy. Look after your Mummy now. Come and see me again soon. Goodbye. Take care. By-ee !"

It was not long after this that the boils had started to erupt. Disgusting gungy sores. From the back of her neck to her insteps. Rosemary was covered in them.

"I think I must be run down," she explained to Dr Chadwick who'd brought both her babies into the world, showing him her neck and arms and tummy. "Can you give me some penicillin or something ? I feel a complete mess."

He thumbed through her medical notes, and then came round and sat on the desk.

"Now, what's the real problem, my girl ?" he asked in his jovial way, pulling her eyelids down to see if she was anaemic.

"It's only the boils," she had insisted. "I'm fine otherwise."

But he wouldn't be fobbed off.

"There's something eating you up, that's what the boils are telling us. And you're not going out of this room until I find out what's at the back of it."

It had been useless protesting that she had no more problems than anyone else. Anyone else with children under foot and a difficult husband, that is. The doctor's kindness and concern had blown the lid off Rosemary's carefully preserved self-control. Her protests were drowned in tears and choked by sobs.

An hour later when at last she emerged from the surgery a

70

sympathetic hush fell on the waiting-room : on the expectant mums, the wheezy old folk, the severely acne-ed teenager. Even the toddler with his thumb in a large bandage stopped running his dinky car round the piles of magazines on the table to stare. Obviously they'd decided between themselves long before Rosemary appeared tear-stained and snivelling that such a lengthy consultation could only mean one thing. That here was someone suffering from some particularly distressing terminal disease.

But they'd been wrong.

What the good doctor had given Rosemary was a prescription that would not only cure her boils, but change her entire life. Ultimately the medicine he handed out to her that long ago afternoon was to give her back her life on a plate.

"Not that I went completely off the rails, mind," she was to tell Maggie afterwards. "After Father, after Pete, for the first time in my life I felt that my body was my own."

This had given her strength. The strength to resist Pete. And a modicum of self-respect.

"Eventually I moved into the spare room. It's true what she said, that Virginia Woolf - to have a room of one's own, your own private space within the hurly-burly of family life, that's what we all need."

"No, he's not a bad husband," she'd tried to explain to Dr Chadwick. "It's silly little things mainly. We've no money, of course. And he's always over at school. He behaves as if we were all a darned nuisance, me and the children. A terrible financial burden. I expect he has enough of kids at work without coming home to another lot. It's always difficult when he's around. Everyone being unnaturally quiet. I daren't think what it's doing to young Billy. I've got to go and see his Form Master next week. He's dropping behind something terrible when he was always in the top two or three. I don't know what's happening to us all."

Oh, dear - she hadn't meant to tell him any of this. But it was too late now.

"And then there's the bed thing . . ."

"Now we're getting to the root of it," the doctor said, passing her a box of Kleenex.

"If I resist him we all suffer. He'll be stroppier than ever next day. Punishing us all. He doesn't beat me or anything." She must be fair to Pete. "But to him marriage seems to mean sex on demand. Sex every night. When he's finished with me I feel dirty. Abused. As if I'd been raped. Sometimes I'm actually sick. Have to rush to the bathroom and throw up. And wash myself out. Wash him out of me. You know. Not that he cares, mind. He's fast asleep the moment he's rolled off me. Satisfied. And oblivious."

She'd been bawling her eyes out by this stage of the consultation. Somehow all the abuse she'd suffered as a child was included in this sorry tale.

"Maybe it's too much to expect a man to understand how gruesome it is to be used like this. But it shrivels you up in the end. Kills something in you."

Dr Chadwick had been prowling up and down in the small consulting room as she wittered on. Now he sat down at his desk again and tore up the prescription he had begun to write.

"Penicillin won't help," he said, looking Rosemary straight in the eye. "What you need, my girl, is a good old-fashioned love affair. And - no - there's no need to look so shocked. I recognise your symptoms quite well. It's not medication you need. But magic. Three quarters of the people who come through this surgery have the same problem. We prescribe vitamin pills, tranquillisers, physiotherapy. But what they need is magic. In your case, a lover. For someone else it might be a new job that's needed. An outside interest. A baby, perhaps. A break from routine. A holiday. It's the drabness that stifles us all. The predictability. The colour has drained out of so many people's lives. That's where your high blood pressure, your heart trouble, your back problems come from. Cancer too, they are beginning to think. Yes, believe me, if there was only a bit more magic around, my surgery would be practically empty. But let's get back to your lover . . ."

"For heaven's sake, you must be joking."

Momentarily Rosemary thought of her body, care-worn, plump, unloved and neglected. And fast approaching forty. A lover ! For Christ's sake ! Dr Chadwick couldn't be serious.

But he was.

"Now the children are older, there's nothing to stop you getting out a bit on your own. Joining something. Taking up some of your old interests again. And when the moment comes (as it will), forget about your nice respectable up-bringing . . ."

Ha ! thought Rosemary, that's a good one !

" . . . Forget about any ludicrous vows you may once have made. Same as all the rest of us, you need a little magic in your life. And as there seems to be none at home, well - you must go out and look for it."

The very idea ! Rosemary remembered thinking. Imagine !

"I wish I could lie on my back by the river all day, laughing at my dreams."

Heavens ! Where was she ? Rosemary sat up with a start, to find Anton crouching beside her on the grass. A golden labrador stretched out nearby, leapt up and started racing round them barking madly.

"I drifted off," she said.

"I know. We've been watching you. It must have been a very vivid dream. I could read it all in your face."

"God ! I hope not ! Here, give me a hand up, Anton. My foot's gone to sleep."

He pulled her up, hugging her tentatively to his crisp blue shirt as he did so.

"Well - I must make a start," she said firmly, deciding to misinterpret this second hug. "I've frittered the entire day away somehow."

"It's nearly five o'clock," he said, agreeing to play it her way. "Too late to start anything now. Walk back to the café with me for a Pernod ?"

But, no - not now, thank you. She was going to do a sketch or two before going home. He turned to wave when he got to the bridge but she chose not to notice though once he was out of sight she quickly gathered herself together and set off for home. Suddenly she was gasping for a large pot of tea. Proper Assam tea that she'd brought with her. And perhaps that delectable apricot pastry that was waiting in the fridge.

Exhausted by her unproductive day, Rosemary took the radio upstairs early intending to listen to Chopin in the dark. But she must have dropped off straight away. The next thing she knew, dawn was breaking, and the bedside light had been burning all night long.

*   *   *

73

Chapter Thirteen

Waiting for the pan of water to boil for her tea, Rosemary opened the door and tip-toed over the wet grass to watch the sun rise across the sea of sunflowers.

She felt intensely alive. It wasn't the sun's rising that she experienced, but the earth's spin. The spin of the planet as her small segment of it moved into the light. While she knew herself to be standing there like the minutest cotton fibre on a spinning tennis ball, yet for a dizzying moment she recognised in her very insignificance the incredible significance of both her own existence and that of every one and every thing with which she shared Mother Earth. For a split second, as the sun cleared the horizon, Rosemary understood the meaning of life. The essence of it shone with blinding clarity in her head. The secret of life was momentarily hers.

Back in bed with her bowl of tea, Rosemary reached up to the beam where she kept Aunt Mary's box. As before, she tipped it onto the quilt, spilling the contents around her - the nine wooden skittles, the yellowing tissue paper, and the card posted to her mother at the end of the war.

'St Julien le Grand,' she read again, trying to discover the source and significance of Aunt Mary's legacy in this faded black and white postcard. In the cluster of lime-washed cottages, the twisting street opening in the foreground onto a tree-lined square. So typically French. So unremarkable. And yet so full of mystery.

Again she studied the clues on the back :

Mme Betsy Fryer
Orchard Cottage
Isle St Agnes
Somerset
Angleterre

The postmark : **Juin 1945 - Perigueux.** And the message : **"Remembering always."**

I must look it up on the map, she thought, more intrigued now than when she first discovered it. And to remind herself, she tucked the post card into a convenient crevice in the richly carved bedhead.

Carefully re-lining the box with the crumpled tissue paper, she popped back into it the Fred and Edward figures. She'd no further need for either of them.

Inspecting the others closely in the bright morning light, she noticed for the first time that here was one with an uncanny resemblance to Pete. He was plumper than his fellows, and in brown doublet and black hose he had very much the air of an artisan. As if to bear this out, in his features was carved that familiar hard-done-to look that Pete had worn for at least the last ten years of their threadbare marriage.

I must be losing my wits, she thought as she ticked off the similarities between this wooden labourer and her ex-husband. I must be injecting something into them. Making them take on this role or that. Mind, it's generally late at night when I talk to them. When I'm woozy and the light's none too good. That could account for it. Yes, this is the first time I've had them out in daylight.

Checking this theory, Rosemary began to pick the remaining mannikins up one by one and study them extra carefully.

But, no. It certainly wasn't imagination. Look at this. The first little fellow that came to hand was - no question, was her Billy.

"Oh, God !" she cried aloud, and clutched him to her. Her son. Her lost son. Blond and beautiful. And lost.

"Why haven't you got a girlfriend, Billy ?" she remembered the twelve year old Betsy asking her six-foot-two brother, when he started at Sixth Form College. "Sarah's brother's going out with Ruthy's big sister, you know. And Lizzy's sister is getting engaged to Ian, and she's only your age."

"Oh, shut up, you. What do you know about it, eh ? A kid like you. Mind your own bloody business."

"You cheeky madam," Rosemary had said. "He's certainly not going to find a girlfriend just to give your gang something to talk about. Have you cleaned your shoes for morning ? Well, off you go. And then I'll hear your French verbs again - OK ?"

"Bloody pansy !" Pete had yelled at him once when instead of watching the football with his father, as had been the custom, Billy sloped off for a long lie in the bath, with his Vivaldi tape and a bowl of cornflakes. "Christ ! When he's finished, the bathroom smells like a beauty parlour. You've ruined the lad, no question."

"Nothing wrong with taking a pride in himself," she'd said, leaping to the boy's defence. "It's normal at this age. I can remember when you were pretty fussy about the way you looked." Not to mention personal hygiene, she added in her head.

Billy had been a quiet boy, avoiding confrontation whenever possible. A loner mostly. He'd worked hard and got a place at Edinburgh. Architecture he was studying. She'd been so proud of him.

"You've not done too badly, William. Considering." Pete, the product of a second rate Teacher Training College, had conceded but without much conviction. "I just hope you can keep up the pace, that's all. It's going to be a long hard slog."

"Be fair, Pete," she'd said, bolder on her son's behalf than on her own. "He's done brilliantly."

"It always amazed me, how he managed to bluff his way through with what was no more than mediocre ability," Pete had announced. Afterwards.

After the sad memorial service at which no more than a handful of Billy's friends had turned up. Two or three from Edinburgh, his contemporaries and his tutor. Two or three from his school days. Poor Billy. Little enough to show for those 24 years of life. The family had supported her, bless them. Davy, travelling all the way down from Northumberland. Aunt Mary, already in her eighties, had been driven over from Somerset by Ben. Doctor Ben.

"Did he ever show a spark of originality, this wonderful son of yours?" The way Pete had gone on that day. That day, for God's sake. "No. He was a hardworking nonentity, I'm afraid. Our Billy. Perhaps now at last you'll admit it."

"Get out of my house," she remembered telling Pete coldly, thankful that the Decree Absolute had come through in time. "Get bloody out!"

It was Pete himself who was the nonentity, of course. He'd been jealous of his quick-witted son. Imagine that - jealous of him! Not only was Billy bright, he was sensitive too. Imaginative and creative. Even as a kid he could draw exquisitely. Fine detailed work, quite distinctive, already.

Oh, Lord - the waste!

Rosemary snuggled deep down in bed with the little figure clutched to her. Oh, Billy . . .

The boy had only been at College a couple of terms when things began to go wrong for him.

She still didn't understand quite what had happened, but in the end he'd been thrown out. It wasn't only his gayness. The place was stiff with it. No, it was the unsavoury company he was keeping. Drop outs, down and outs, male prostitutes. And there were drugs involved too, she heard from his tutor, Dr Smithson, at the Memorial Service.

Billy did come home once during that anxious time. To collect the last of his things.

"Don't worry about me, Mother," he'd said, loading his childhood into a taxi. "At last I've found a friend. A real friend. I'll be in touch."

And just as the taxi was pulling away, he'd let the window down to call to her, "Why didn't you stand up to the bugger, Mum ? Why did you let him get away with it ?"

And that was the last she was ever to see of this sad young man. This cuckoo chick. This changeling. Her Billy.

"He doesn't look like any of us," the family had pointed out on the rare occasions they'd seen the child. "So fair. So tall and lanky. He's certainly not like our side. And he's not like Pete's either."

"He's certainly not like his Grandfather Fryer."

"Well that's something to be thankful for !" Rosemary remembered saying to Maggie, once everything was out in the open. By then they were able to laugh about it. Almost.

"Funnily enough, he does remind me of someone," Rosemary's brother Davy had said when he saw the lad for the first time in years at somebody's wedding. One of the cousin's. Julia's probably. Henry's youngest. Yes, that was it. Julia was married, when was it ? - in the summer that Billy took his A Levels.

Rosemary could see them all now, milling around the striped marquee on Henry's lawn. Julia was being given the full works by her doting father, in spite of the fact that she and Marcus had been sharing a flat in London for a year and more, quite openly. They only decided to legalise things when he was offered a posting in Saudi Arabia, a three year contract with a civil engineering firm. Married, she could go out with him.

Davy, now Senior Partner in his Hexham veterinary practice,

stood quietly apart, watching all the to-ing and fro-ing among the family, which with husbands and wives and offspring and a sprinkling of the next generation numbered forty-something.

"A funny bunch, aren't we, Rosie !" Davy had said, drawing her to him affectionately as they lined up for fruit salad. "And such a strong family likeness running through the whole tribe. Have you seen that little grandson of Frankie's ?"

The toddler in question was sitting on Aunt Mary's lap sharing a bowl of ice cream with her.

"Heavens !" Rosemary suddenly realised how many generations were gathered there at the wedding feast. "He must be Aunt Mary's Great Great Nephew. Think of that !"

"Let's get some air," Davy said, steering her out into the garden. "Henry may be a highly respected barrister, but he's got some bloody boring friends if this lot are anything to go by."

They plonked themselves down on the trim grassy bank overlooking the tennis court.

Billy came out of the house just then, looking pale and delicate and beautiful, in an astonishing straw hat he'd brought back from the school trip to Italy at Easter. He'd waved at his mother, nodded at his Uncle Davy, and wandered off into the vegetable garden by himself.

"Apart from that young man," Davy had said, following his earlier train of thought.

"How do you mean ?"

"Your Billy - he's a right enigma. Must be a throwback, I guess. Unless you're keeping something from us all, Rosie. He's not the milkman's, by any chance? Come on, you can tell your big brother."

"Oh shut up, you ! I was a faithful little wife from Day One. For my sins. Our Billy's as much family as I am. And don't you go stirring it up for me with your genetic speculations or . . ."

"Mummy !" Bridesmaid Betsy came dancing over to join them and save the day. "That little Amy has spilt Ribena all down her bridesmaid's dress and Julia's mummy is really cross with her and she says we've all got to go indoors and have a rest but I don't have rests do I ? Tell Aunt Dolly, Mummy. Tell her. Please. I don't have to go in for a rest. At my age ! Tell her, Mum."

"No doubt about this one, anyway," said Davy, picking the child up and swinging her high in the air so that her delicate daffodil dress flew out around her like something from a Ken Russell film.

"A Fryer through and through, bless her cotton socks."

"Julia's turned out a beauty . . ."

"And a bit of a rebel, by the sound of it, much to everyone's surprise."

"Brainy though. She's really going places, that young Julia. You know where they met, she and Marcus ?"

"No."

"Mensa. For what it's worth."

"Really ?"

"Not that an IQ means much. It's the immeasurables that count in life, wouldn't you agree - originality, dedication, determination . . ."

"Creativity, sensitivity, warmth . . ."

"And there's no way of measuring these . . ."

"Except life itself - that's the real test, isn't it."

"It's not what you're given - brains, beauty or whatever. It's what you do with your gifts that counts."

"Right - what you make of what you've got. Great or small."

"Henry's certainly made the most of himself. I don't think I've seen either of them since Mother's funeral. With him being so much older than me, he was more like an uncle."

"Not the easiest chap to get along with," said Davy, "but highly successful nevertheless. I've heard it said that he's in line for elevation."

"Elevation ?"

"Our brother Henry will probably finish up on the bench. As a judge."

"A judge ! Dolly knew what she was doing when she chose Henry, then. She'll be unbearable when the time comes. She's bad enough already."

"Right. In her Georgian mansion."

"With Cook and the daily woman."

"And Williams in the garden."

"Everything so nice, don't you know."

"Everything bloody perfect."

"He's been working towards it for years, mind, Rosie."

"*She* has, don't you mean ?"

"They have together. She's in with the Cathedral nobs. And he's a big noise with the Masons."

"The Masons ? Henry ? My stars !"

"Oh, yes. They've always done all the right things. And it clearly works." Davy spread his arms wide to embrace his brother's assets : the elegant old house, the well-kept lawns running down to the river, the high wall around the kitchen garden, the fashionable and distinguished company gathered together to celebrate Julia's wedding.

"Come on, poppet," Rosemary said, taking Betsy's hand. "I'm feeling more inadequate by the minute. Let's go and find Aunt Mary. Get things back in perspective."

"She's gone to look at the vegetables with our Billy," Betsy said. "Look - there they are. Coo-ee ! Aunt Mary ! Wait for me !" And off she ran, her chestnut curls and her yellow skirt flying around her.

"Aunt Mary's very fond of Billy," Rosemary had explained to Davy, as she pulled him to his feet too. "She always has been. And he's fond of her. I sometimes think she's the only one he feels comfortable with. Funny, isn't it."

"She always had a way with the young ones. She treated us with, well, let's say, with respect, didn't she ? We were darned lucky we had her, Rosie. When you think of Father. And poor pathetic Mother. Oh, dear !"

For a moment, Rosie had a compelling desire to tell this strong sane brother of hers about Father. But somehow she couldn't. Not here. Not now. What if she were to weep in front of all Dolly's nice friends ? What if Davy were to rave ?

"Poor Mother," she said instead. "I don't think I ever told you, but when I went over to see her in the Nursing Home that last week - remember ? She kept singing. Mother. Singing. Wasn't that odd. She was quite helpless physically and seemed to have no idea where she was or who she was. I don't think she recognised me, but I stayed beside her just the same. As far as I could tell, she thought I was a Social Worker or something. A time or two she said, 'It's very kind of you to call. I hope I'm not being a bother.' Very polite. As if I was a stranger."

"Poor little Mother," Davy said, covering his face with his hands.

"Totally confused. And then this singing."

Rosemary remembered their mother's voice, light and childish, as she sang songs of her childhood, songs of her youth. War songs. Hymns. French folk songs. There was no stopping her.

"Mother ! Sh ! You'll wake all the old ladies up. You must settle down and go to sleep. Mother !"

But as she crept away, heavily pregnant with Betsy, to spend another unhappy night alone in their childhood home, Rosemary could hear Mother singing to herself again. And there was something almost joyful about the song, strange to say.

"Au clair de la lune, mon ami Pierrot . . ."

"I'm sorry about Mother's singing," she said guiltily to the Ward Sister as she slipped away to the car park. "She's never sung in her life."

"Don't worry. These things effect us all in different ways. She's back in her childhood. In the happier times. She sings rather sweetly, we've been saying. Let her sing while she can. The others are past noticing. We'll ring you if there's any change. Goodnight, my dear. You'll be in tomorrow as usual ?"

"I didn't see her at the end," Davy said. "She was taken ill while we were out in Canada, remember. I flew home for the funeral. I'm glad you told me about the singing, Rosie. Maybe all the sad times were wiped away, and . . ."

"And she was young and free and happy again."

"I hope so. Oh, I do hope so."

Later, when the happy couple had been taken to the airport, and the family were all preparing to drive back into their separate worlds, Davy said it again, leaping out of his car when they were all safely strapped in, Davy and Stella and their three teenagers in the back. Leaping out and rushing across to Rosemary as she was saying goodbye to Aunt Mary who was getting a lift back to Somerset with Frankie and John on their way to Plymouth.

"Rosie !" he'd called. "What we were saying. Billy. He does remind me of someone. Someone from way back. It'll come to me shortly. I'll tell you when it does. I can almost remember already."

"Oh, Davy !" Aunt Mary had said, shaking her head in despair. "He always was one to worry away at something till he'd found the answer."

But there had been no answer for Billy.

No answer except . . .

He'd gone to California when they threw him out of university. To a country where he could live freely and joyfully with his Real Friend. A year later the friend had died of AIDS. Billy had phoned.

"Oh, Mum - I don't know how I'm going to cope without him. He was my whole life."

"Come home, Billy, love. Have a holiday at home. Give yourself a chance to recover, sort out the future. It's different now that Dad's left. We wouldn't intrude on you, Betsy and I. She's turned out so sane and strong and sensible. You'll be able to talk to Betsy. Come home where you belong, love."

"I have to stay here. See to everything for Phil. Afterwards - well, maybe I'll come home for a while afterwards. I'll see. But I'm glad you asked me, Mum. I'm really glad you asked me."

And having made all the arrangements for Phil's funeral, and seen his ashes scattered on the ocean, Billy had gone down to the beach and swum off into the Pacific sunset. He'd left a note that the Los Angeles police sent on to her :

'Sorry, Mum, but without Phil there's no point going on.'

"Marie-Rose !" There was Hugo banging at the door, and his Erna barking, and the morning half gone while she lay in bed with her memories.

"I could see you were not yet up," he said, when she hung out of the bedroom window. "Are you ill ?"

"I'm coming right down to make us a big pot of coffee, mon ami. Tout de suite."

"It is the day for shearing my lambs. You said you wanted to watch - remember."

She wanted to watch him, yes. She wanted to help him. She wanted to capture the operation on her sketch pad.

How her Billy would have revelled in the life she'd found here among the fields of sunflowers, she thought, pulling on her jeans. Now he would have been a wonderful companion. If only he had allowed himself recovery time.

Oh, Billy.

And opening the window wide and leaving the bed to air, Rosemary went down to help Hugo Forêt with the shearing.

* * *

82

Chapter Fourteen

"There's something I want to ask you, Marie-Rose," Hugo said when the shearing was finished, and his six adolescent lambs were frisking around their mothers in the steep meadow below the farmstead, thankful to have their curly coats off. "On Friday I have to go down to the Dordogne. To take a party of academics round one or two of the Grottes."

"Grottes ?"

"The painted caves, you know. At Les Eyzies. With the pre-historic paintings. You must have heard of them. They are world famous."

"I have. Of course I have. But why you, when you're so far away ?"

"I told you about my post at Bordeaux, didn't I ?"

"Yes, yes - I see. You take parties round because of your work as an Art Historian ?"

"That's right. We used to organise regular visits to the caves during my time at the University. And the Department still calls on me two or three times a year. For my special groups. All of them real experts in the field. Or if one of the other Guides drops out."

"I keep meaning to take a trip down there myself," she found herself saying.

"That's what I want to talk to you about."

They were sitting in the shade of the mulberry tree beside the barn. With glasses of Pernod.

"I was going to ask if you would like to come along with me. If you can spare the time."

"Oh, no. I couldn't barge in on your party. I'll drive down there myself one of these days. But it was a kind suggestion."

"It wasn't kind at all. For one thing, it would be a great help if you were with me, as most of this particular group are American and I hoped you might lend a hand with the commentary. My English is not half as good as your French."

"Oh - well - that's different. If you are sure I would be a help, then I'd love to come along. Thank you, Hugo."

"The other point is that if you don't come with me on this trip you are very unlikely to get into the caves at all."

"Why's that then ? It's a longish way, I know, but I could get there and back in a day if I set off good and early."

"It's not that. You could get down there, true. But you couldn't get into the caves. They are no longer open to the public, you see. Because of deterioration and all that. Atmospheric stress. In the hundred or so years since they were discovered, atmospheric pollution has been steadily eating into the paintings. Now the Authorities have been forced to close the caves to the public before the paintings are totally destroyed. Oh, pardonez-moi. I'm so passionate about the subject that I burst into my Public Address Mode at the slightest provocation."

"Good God ! No need to apologise. I'm touched that you're inviting me along. Otherwise I wouldn't have had a chance to see the paintings, by the sound of it. I simply hadn't realised."

"It will mean an overnight stay in Bordeaux."

"But your wife - doesn't she want to go with you ?"

"Sadly, no - she's never been interested in these things, Yvonne."

They were to leave early on Friday morning, driving down to Les Eyzies in the Dordogne to meet up there with the party from Bordeaux at lunchtime.

"If I was going alone, I would drive back into Bordeaux with the Americans after we'd seen the caves. They always lay on a wonderful Dinner that night, the last night of their Conference."

"Oh, look . . ." she began, thinking her presence would be an embarrassment to him.

"No, listen !" he said, seeing the way her mind was working. "I shall be delighted to take you along to the Dinner with me, as my guest. They put us up in student accommodation on campus - single rooms, it's basic but comfortable. That's if you don't mind spending so much time away from home."

Home, she thought. That's nice. I do feel at home here. Comfortable and settled.

"But the farm, the animals . . . ?"

His brother-in-law had agreed to look after things in his absence. It was all arranged.

"It's a long drive. I would like to take it in easy stages. Stop for breakfast en route. Can you be ready for five-thirty, Marie-Rose ? Is that too early ?"

They had coffee and croissants at Angoulême. And stopped again to stretch their legs at Brantôme.

The landscape was changing. It was hillier and thickly wooded. There were still odd patches of sunflowers but in clearings in the forest here. Bright splodges among the trees.

In nearly every farmyard, nearly every patch of woodland there were flocks of geese.

"*Foie gras* country," Hugo explained. "We'll be sampling it at lunchtime."

Slowing up as they drove through a small and unremarkable village, Rosemary suddenly had a feeling of déjà-vu which was so powerful that for a moment she thought she might black out.

They'd driven through the place and out the other side before she could speak.

"That village, did you notice its name ?"

"There - look. On the road-side. St Julien le Something-or-Other," he said pointing to the YOU HAVE JUST PASSED THROUGH sign on the verge. And a mile or two later, "Pourquoi ? Do you to want to go back and look round ?"

But Rosemary couldn't say. She felt all kind of numb and dizzy. Yet it had looked such an ordinary little place. They'd driven through half-a-dozen already today that were almost identical. A cluster of modest houses on a crossroad most of them in need of a coat of white-wash. A shabby looking church. A square shaded by plain trees. Nothing exceptional. And yet . . .

It niggled away at her while they drove deeper and deeper into the Dordogne. Now cliffs of sandstone towered above the road obviously smoothed and sculpted and hollowed out by ocean waves.

"But, surely, we're miles inland. And high above sea level !" Rosemary exclaimed in astonishment.

"Look," he told her, slowing the car. "You can see the various high water marks. The prehistoric tide marks. The whole area was once beside the sea. All these caves for which it is so famous were eaten out by water. Some by rivers and underground water courses, others by the tide."

Sometimes the road ran right underneath a great shelf or overhang carved in billowing and mysterious shapes by those distant breakers.

Every now and again there was a sign up : **Grotte Prehistorique**. Sometimes a stall selling souvenirs.

"But you said the public were no longer allowed in," she said.

"Ah, these are merely the fringe attractions. Perhaps this cave has one faint painting in it. The next none at all. And even then the paintings in them are not always genuine. There's a good living to be made out of the tourist. Rock samples, fossils perhaps. Guided tours, refreshments, postcards."

"Postcards !" Rosemary said. "That's it !" The postcard in Aunt Mary's box. That's why I recognised it, she thought. "St Julien le *what* ?"

"St Julien le, le Grand, I think it was. But it's hardly worth getting excited about, ma chère. For heaven's sake. It looked a very ordinary sort of place, so far as I can remember."

"Sorry," she said. "I'm just so thankful I can place it, that's all. Hey, look at this !"

The car swung onto a tree-lined bridge (A *tree-lined bridge !* Surely not !) across a deep river gorge.

"The Dordogne ?"

"Mais non," he laughed. "The Dordogne is a great wide waterway. This is no more than a mountain stream."

They drew up outside a promising looking hotel with tables on the terrace under a canopy of vines. From here they could watch the traffic weaving across the bridge through the criss-cross shadows of the lime trees.

"Just time for an apéritif before we meet up with the others," he said.

"I'm so glad you asked me along, Hugo," she said. And it suddenly dawned on her how distinguished he looked in his Sunday best. Until now she'd mostly seen him pottering about the farm in dungarees and wellies. "Come on - I'm paying for the drinks. No, no arguing. It's been a grand trip so far, never mind the caves."

"It would have been a dreary ride on my own."

They sat in friendly silence, sipping their cool pastis. Watching the world crossing the bridge.

"That looks like our lot," he said, as a coach crawled across in front of them. "Best be making our way to the rendez-vous."

There were about twenty in the party of academics. Most of them American. And to Rosemary, surprisingly youthful.

"Ah, Hugo - good to see you again, man !"

They all seemed to know him. And respect him.

"At last we get to meet your wife, eh ?"

"No, no. This is a friend from England, Rosemary Richardson. An artist herself. Of some distinction."

"Oh, rubbish !" she said.

But they took his word for it, hugging her to them, gathering her unquestioningly into their erudite midst.

Lunch had been booked in advance. A long trestle table was set out ready for them in a shady courtyard. It was a noisy meal. There was excellent potage, followed by the local pâté, long sticks of crusty bread and a huge bowl of green salad. And an endless supply of red wine.

"Alors, time to be moving," said Hugo, when the coffee pot had circulated among the peach stones for the second time. And he shepherded them out to the car park.

The cave they were looking for was a mile or two up the road. The transport was left in a fenced-off space on the bank of the stream, and the party waded through the lush meadow awash with wild flowers, blue and pink, white and yellow.

Then came the climb. To get to the mouth of the cave they had to clamber up a steep path carved out of the limestone by the look of it. In some places wooden steps had been built. There was a stout railing all the way to the top, protecting them from the sheer drop to their right as they climbed.

"You shouldn't have given us such a good lunch, Hugo !"

"We should have stuck to the Perrier."

"Someone's going to have to carry me."

Most of the party saved their breath for the climb.

"I darned well hope it's going to be worth it, Hugo - I'm getting too old for mountaineering."

It was worth it. Rosemary would have climbed another thousand feet to see it. Happily.

The experts were silenced by what they saw. Rosemary was awed. Over-awed, in fact. Stunned.

Cassette players with headphones had been handed out before they began the climb.

"I'm sorry about the light," Hugo said in a whisper that ran round the walls of the subterranean chamber, bouncing and magnifying as it went.

The light was dim. It seemed to operate automatically, coming on just ahead of them as they moved through the cave, and switching itself off behind them.

Some areas of wall painting were protected behind glass screens, but most of the decorated surfaces were too bumpy and billowy.

"Notice how cleverly the artist used the natural form of the limestone," Hugo whispered.

It was true. Very often, a knobble had been incorporated into the picture as the head of a bison, the rump of mammoth, the shoulders of a bull. Hollows were used with similar skill to give a three dimensional quality to the space between antlers, a spindliness to the legs of deer.

This was the work of genuine artists, Rosemary realised. People with a feeling for balance and drama, with a deep understanding of the animals they depicted so vividly, a respect for their various strengths. And for the kinship of all, Mankind included.

Listening to the English commentary on their headphones they shuffled through the passages and galleries in spell-bound silence. Once or twice Hugo signalled back that here was something of extra-special interest.

Rosemary was at the tail end of the group, sweeping the experts along in front of her. She saw Hugo stop and point to a spot on the wall, holding up his left hand with the fingers splayed as he did so. By the time she reached the place everyone else had moved on into the next gallery. She scanned the richly coloured mural for the item of special interest. And there it was - the hand-print.

The wall here was too knobbly to be protected by glass. Without realising what she was doing, Rosemary knelt down and somehow found her own hand planted over the artist's. And the amazing thing was that her hand matched the hand of that cave painter. Matched it exactly.

"Marie-Rose !" Hugo had come back to find her. "Are you ill ? Did you fall ? There - let me help you."

"I'm fine. Honestly. I crouched down to look at the hand-print, and then the light went out."

"You'd got left behind somehow. I hadn't realised. Thank goodness you're OK." He helped her to her feet. The light was on again now. "Come on, take my hand. You're looking wobbly. They'll be through the last stretch by now and out in the open. And thinking we've both been swallowed up, I guess."

The climb down to the meadow where the coach was parked was almost as difficult as the ascent had been.

"Gets you in the knees. doesn't it !"

"It's tomorrow we'll suffer, mark my words."

"We'll go on ahead in the car," Hugo explained, counting them into the coach. "Dinner is at eight. See you all in the Bar before that."

"It was a great trip, Hugo !"

"Wonderful, man !"

"Must be just about the best of all the French caves."

"Thank you . . ."

"Merci beaucoup . . ."

"See you later."

It was a long drive to Bordeaux. Rosemary dozed off a time or two.

"Sorry. Don't want to miss the countryside. I can't keep my eyes open."

"Don't worry. It's been a long day. I'll be asleep myself if I'm not careful."

"How old are the paintings ?" she asked him.

"Palaeolithic," he said. "Early Stone Age."

"Early Stone Age ?"

"Thirty-five thousand years. Maybe older."

"Thirty-five thousand !" Rosemary was stunned. "I'd no idea . . ."

They drove in silence for a good many miles. Indeed he thought she was asleep again. Then Rosemary held her left hand up against the light, fingers splayed wide, examining it in silhouette against the setting sun.

"I'd no idea . . ." she said again. "That hand-print was the same as mine. The very same. I somehow imagined they would have had primitive hands." More like apes, perhaps. Fleshy. Coarse. With thick pads on finger tips and palm. "But that hand, the hand of that artist was no different from my own."

"Hope you didn't touch it, Marie-Rose. Desecrate it."

"No. No, I didn't touch it, Your Honour !" she said. But it wasn't true. She had touched it. Indeed she'd crouched down and pressed her own hand onto the other. The signature of that artist. She had felt she had to. Felt compelled to. There had been no choice. And her own hand had matched it. Perfectly.

"Here we are," he said, as they turned in at the imposing gates of the University. "And we've time for baths and a drink before the others arrive. A quiet drink on our own."

"The head-phones," she said, suddenly confused. "Didn't you know about the head-phones ? There was no need for me to come after all, lovey. They had their English commentaries on tape."

"Let's say, I wasn't sure they'd have head-phones," he said, opening the car door for her. "I was afraid you wouldn't agree to come. I had to think of some plausible inducement."

"Oh, Hugo ! And I believed every word of it !"

"I really wanted you to come on this trip with me, Marie-Rose, believe me . . ."

"And believe me, I'm glad you persuaded me. Thank you, thank you, my dear." And dropping her overnight bag on the University steps, she reached up and hugged him.

* * *

Chapter Fifteen

It was very late before anyone got to bed that night. After a splendid dinner with mussels and pork and strawberry gateaux, and toasts and speeches, they danced. Boy, did they dance - these erudite American academics !

"Everyone onto the floor now ! Come on, you two - get out there and dance !"

"I haven't danced for years," Rosemary protested. "I've two left feet. Honestly !"

"And I've two right ones . . ." said Hugo, ushering her out onto the floor.

The music was wild and insistent. The sort of stuff that Betsy had played as she swotted for her A Levels.

"Betsy ! Turn it down, can't you !" she'd yelled time and again. To no effect.

"Sorry, Ma - I can't think without it. You want me to get good grades, yes ? This is the price I'm afraid."

For weeks the house had pulsated madly. Rock, Pop and Reggae blaring from the bathroom, the kitchen, Betsy's bedroom, the garden . . .

"For God's sake, girl - we never had this with Billy. Do you want to drive your mother crazy !"

And now the music was driving her crazy again. But in a different way altogether.

"I tell you, I'm a complete fool on the dance floor, Hugo."

But it wasn't true.

With the sedate one-two-three, one-two-three routine, yes. The old slow-slow-quick-quick-slow. Then sure enough she'd been hopeless. Tripping over her own feet and her partner's with the strain of keeping time.

"Girls ! Girls ! Come along now. Try to take it seriously." Poor Miss Pickwick, desperately attempting to give the Fifth Formers a smattering of savoir faire in the gym on wet Games afternoons. "Rosie ! Sit out, girl ! I've never seen such a lack of co-ordination."

Disco dancing was a different kettle of fish entirely.

To her astonishment Rosemary discovered that with the music pounding in her ears (**By the rivers of Babylon, where we sat down . . .**), she suddenly became totally brilliantly co-ordinated. Without a thought for the distinguished company, how ridiculous she must look, the embarrassment she might be causing Hugo, she found herself dancing.

With total abandon this middle-aged creature, plump and plain and awkward as she had always seen herself, joined the Americans in the rhythm of the dance. With them she whirled and leapt. She kicked her legs in the air. She swayed and sang. She allowed the music to flow through her arms, her hands, her fingers. She threw herself into it with careless rapture.

Her response to the rhythm was primitive and spontaneous.

"Can I have this dance ?" asked Rupert the grey-beard from New York State.

"Come on, there, kid - dance with your Uncle Bobby from Tennessee ?"

"Hey now, darling - how about doing a turn with me. Back in Baltimore . . ."

Never mind Baltimore. Let's get out on the floor, man !

Suddenly every one was asking her to dance. Not that she danced WITH her partner. Not in the old Ballroom sense: clutching him grimly while frantically trying to predict his footwork, tripping over, stepping on his highly polished toes, losing the flow in the struggle to co-operate.

Nothing like that at this dance. Yes, she'd get to her feet with Uncle Bobby, Hugo, the Doctor of Philosophy from L.A. She'd get to her feet with any of them. But once on the floor, once the music got a hold of her, Rosemary was off. On her own. Whirling alone, wild and free.

"Gee ! You are so darned sexy," said one of the younger Archaeologists misunderstanding her intoxication. "How if we escape out onto the terrace, huh ? Get a little better acquainted ?"

She very quickly lost him on the floor.

"**Una Paloma Blanca . . .**" What a tune ! "**I'm just a bird in the sky . . . over the mountains I fly . . . no-one can take my freedom away . . . da-da-da da-da-da daaa.**"

That's me, she thought, whirling back to their table.

Una paloma blanca. As free as a bird in the sky.

"Thought you said you weren't a dancer," Hugo said when the party finally began to disperse.

"This was different."

He put a friendly arm on her shoulder as they set off across the quadrangle to the residential block.

"Hey, you guys - not going to bed, surely ? We're staying up to watch the sun rise. Why not join us ?"

"Not me," Rosemary said. "I'm knackered." One way or another, it had been quite a day. "I'm off to my bed."

"That's too bad, then. It was a great day, huh !"

"A great party."

"Goodnight !"

"Goodnight ! Goodnight !"

"God, I need a bath !" she said when they reached their landing.

"Another bath ?"

"That was hot work. I'm sweating like - like the proverbial pig."

"Watch it. I've a soft spot for porkers."

"So have I, now I come to think of it," she said, remembering a rainy day and a letter from England, and a small bundle of piglet snuffling contentedly on her knee.

"It's been a wonderful day," she told him unlocking her bedroom door. "From start to finish. Quite perfect. I'm so glad you persuaded me to come." And again she reached up and kissed him affectionately on each cheek. "Goodnight, my dear !"

She was disgustingly hot and smelly after all that. Soaking in the tub, Rosemary could hear that some of the group were indeed still out of doors, wandering around the garden, laughing, whispering. Staying up to greet the dawn on this the last morning of their Bordeaux Conference. Clean and sweet again, she stood quite naked at the open window tinglingly alive in the welcome chill.

"Marie-Rose . . ." There was a timid knock on the door.

She grabbed her dressing-gown.

"Oh, Hugo. You gave me quite a fright. Come in, love. Come in."

He stood there in his pyjamas, awkward and shy.

"There's something I want to tell you, chérie . . ." And in the darkness he came across to the window, and diffidently, tenderly took her in his arms. "Ma chère, my sweet Marie-Rose."

"No !" she said, as he started kissing her neck, stroking her hair. "Mais non !"

He didn't persist but lent against the window frame, his face in his hands.

"Alors, mon ami - qu'est ce qu'il y a ?" And she pushed him firmly into the chair by the student's desk, the only chair in the room, and wrapping her cotton robe firmly around her she perched on the desk facing him.

He'd loved her from the very first, he said. And the more he got to know her the more he'd grown to love her.

"But - but Hugo you have a wife."

And now at last he told her about his wife.

"We married young, Yvonne and I. It was a big mistake. We're both Catholics. There was nothing to be done but stick it out. There's been no warmth in it for years. Since our son was born probably and he's nearly 35 now. I've been faithful to her in spite of everything. My work became my life. I learnt to live without - well, without love. No, it's not just sex I'm talking about. It's gentleness, tenderness, understanding, friendship. I'd come to accept that I would never know any of these things. And then you drove into the farmyard."

She hadn't realised, of course. She'd been too pre-occupied with her own dismal affairs.

"No," she said again, when he'd told her everything. "Please - no. It would be a mistake. It would alter, it would spoil everything."

At one time I would have leapt into bed with him, she realised. Hungrily.

"I'm sorry, but it's too soon, too unexpected." She was still trying to come to terms with the Edward thing. "Forgive me, but no. Not yet, anyway."

"I understand, ma petite. I respect you for your decision. But . . ." and he reached out and gripped her hand, "but could I spend the night with you ? No hanky-panky. I give you my word. Please let me sleep here beside you. Please."

It wasn't much to ask.

The bed was narrow, but it didn't matter. With a deep sigh he stretched out against the wall. After the briefest hesitation Rosemary climbed in beside him, turning her back to him to nestle down in his arms.

"I've been dreaming about this," he whispered sleepily. "Oh, how I've longed to have you in my arms."

And squeezing her tight against him, he suddenly fell asleep, his grip relaxing as he began to snore quietly in a comforting kind of way.

Rosemary did not sleep.

The things Hugo had told her swirled round and round in her head. To be honest, she was surprised at herself. In the past, she had to admit, she'd probably have engineered it. Weeks ago. Without a qualm. Perhaps at last she was learning a little sense. It's easy enough starting a relationship. Living with it is the problem. Finishing it. She was not ready for all that again. Not just yet. Not till she'd recovered from the last lot.

And of course there was Madame Forêt to consider.

She was ashamed to think how many times in the past few years she'd jumped into bed with Tom, Dick or Harry. So lightly, so casually. Once or twice she'd regretted it afterwards. Usually it had been fun. Nothing serious. Friendly, comforting and fun.

She must have dozed off because the next thing she knew the sky was bright with pearly light and apart from the dawn chorus all was quiet down on the lawn.

Without disturbing Hugo, who seemed to be sleeping like a baby, she crept out of bed and along to the bathroom. When she got back, he'd gone. Slipped away to his own room for fear of embarrassment, she guessed, further rejection.

Now she'd seen him in this other role, as distinguished academic, Rosemary realised who he reminded her of. George. Poor old George. Another academic. Another sad lonely husband.

"Fancy bumping into each other again," George had said when, spotting him at the bar of The Royal Oak that January lunchtime, she'd called over to him to join her in the ingle-nook beside the log fire. "I sometimes treat myself to a quick one on a Wednesday. While Florrie's having her hair done."

After that, they'd make a point of meeting there, in the bar of The Royal Oak. On a Wednesday. When it was possible.

"I really enjoy this," he was to say to her now and then. "It's

95

about the only hour I ever have to myself." He was heavily married, was George.

It was their innocent secret.

"Do you know," he said on that last Wednesday, "I've told you things I've never told anyone. Funny, that. And we scarcely know each other."

They'd first met at the Cathedral Carol Service. They'd just happened to sit next to one another, that was all. He'd had this frightful outburst of coughing, poor man. And by chance Rosemary had had some fruit-gums in her pocket which had saved the day. Streaming out into the frosty Close afterwards with the seasonal magic still entrancing them both, he'd insisted on buying her a cup of coffee, and at that time of night The Royal Oak had been the best option.

Now it seemed as if they had been sharing a drink in there for years, though it was only a matter of weeks, she realised afterwards. Seven weeks, that was all.

"We've been happy enough," George told her, that last Wednesday. "Don't misunderstand me. Florrie's a love. We've been lucky. By most standards, we've been lucky. It's just that . . ." and to Rosemary's alarm he started weeping quietly into his bitter.

The pub was busy. Noisy. Nobody noticed the sad little drama in the corner.

"Dear George," she remembered saying, uselessly. And stroking his heavily veined hand.

"Once," he said, as he blew his nose, "once long ago I was staying with my grandparents. On the Yorkshire coast, they lived. Near Whitby. It must have been in my student days. I'd have gone over there from college. From Leeds. For a weekend, probably. I was only young."

"Is that seat taken ?" A smart young couple pushed in beside them, squeezing her up against George. For the first time - the only time, as it turned out - he put his arm around her shoulders.

"I always wake early. Still do. That morning I was up and out before dawn, following the cliff-top path along beside a high brick wall. Twelve foot high. Maybe more. I discovered afterwards it was the boundary wall of some great estate. It went on and on. For ever. I'd brought a hunk of Gran's wonderful bread and dripping with me - home-made bread, rich dripping off the Sunday joint. And a flask of tea. I found a good spot, and settled down with my back against the wall, the cliffs dropping away below, the sea sparkling in the early sunlight. And suddenly, suddenly this music started. From nowhere. Guitar music. And obviously played by a master. Albinoni it was or one of his contemporaries. And unbearably sweet. Haunting."

She didn't interrupt but let him ramble on.

"I sat there enraptured. Leaning up against the wall, life suddenly seemed so beautiful. So inexplicable. And full of such endless promise. The way it does to the young. I remember," and his voice was shaking, "I remember that I sat there and wept. Just like today, I found myself weeping my heart out. Heaven knows why. I'm sorry to be such a silly old fool . . ." And the tears started again.

Although this was against their unspoken rule, Rosemary had gone over and got them another drink. Brandy this time.

"I have enjoyed our friendship," he said, when they'd battled their way through the lunchtime crowd at the bar, and were shaking hands outside as usual before going their separate ways. "Goodbye, dear girl. And God bless you."

He must have known somehow, Rosemary had realised afterwards. He must have known.

The following Wednesday when he didn't turn up she thought nothing of it. Florrie's hair appointment must have been changed. Perhaps they'd decided to drive over and see their daughter in Sussex.

But that weekend she saw it in the paper :

George Bakewell, the distinguished Archaeologist, died peacefully in his sleep in his 81st year . . . survived by his wife Florence and their daughter Mary.

Archaeologist. Rosemary had forgotten that. George would have enjoyed yesterday's trip. He would have been perfectly at home among the distinguished academics at last night's party.

Looking down from her window now onto the deserted campus of Bordeaux University, Rosemary noticed the early light shimmering on the surface of the outdoor swimming pool. Grabbing her towel, she crept along the dormitory corridor and down the three flights of stairs, across the lawn where evidence of the academics' late night frolics lay about among the rose bushes - wine bottles mostly. With a hasty look round to check that she was not being spied on from the residential block, Rosemary threw her robe over a bench, and plunged into the pool. As she turned at the deep end to do another length, the sun rose in splendour in the cloudless sky. Feeling quite bold suddenly, she clambered out and climbed up to the top board. Naked, she stood with arms outstretched for a swallow dive. And plunged into the fiery water that now reflected the fierceness of the sunrise.

Earth, air, fire, water, Rosemary thought, with a shiver of excitement. All in a moment she'd travelled from earth, through air, to pierce the flaming surface of the pool and enter the clear blue water. Wow!

No-one had witnessed her early swim. After steaming bowls of milky coffee with their bread and jam, it was time to set off for home.

"See you next year, then,"

"Sure. Great conference."

"And the cave paintings . . . !"

"Aw gee - they really were something !"

It was a long drive back, and late afternoon before they drew up outside the farmhouse. To her surprise, there was no awkwardness between them after Hugo's declaration. Rosemary dozed off more than once on the way. He played tapes, and now and then told her about the town or village they were going through, about the crops, the history, the river beside which it was built. Everything between them was perfectly proper. Perfectly normal. Bless him for that, she thought.

"I'll make us a cup of tea," Rosemary said when they reached the farmyard.

"No, no thanks. I'd better check the stock and get off home."

"It was a splendid trip," she said. "I'm so glad you persuaded me to go. Thank you, Hugo, my dear." And she risked giving him a peck on the cheek.

That night, tired as she was after the excitement of the trip and the long drive home, Rosemary was unable to sleep. After tossing about for what seemed like hours, she got the Edwardian brick box down from the beam above her head, and once again spread the little wooden figures around her on the quilt.

Yes, here was Edward. And - oh my goodness, Father ! It hadn't struck her before. And bloody Pete. This one was her darling Billy. This cheeky little fellow was surely old Sixsmith, with his lecherous grin. And good heavens, how come she hadn't noticed before, **this one** looked terribly like Mr Forêt. Hugo Forêt.

Before snuggling down again, she had another look at that mysterious postcard with the faded photograph of - yes ! Of St Julien Le Grand. She had indeed recognised it on the way south yesterday. No wonder it had given her goose-bumps, finding herself 'in the picture', as it were.

It looked a fairly nondescript place, with a modest market square, a stumpy church, an old chestnut tree with a circular bench around it. Funny how fascinated she was by it. Funny how she'd reacted to it as they drove through. Again Rosemary asked herself how the devil the postcard could have come to be in her box of nine-pins. Why it had come to her ? Who on earth would have been writing to her mother from central France ? At the end of the War ?

The pendulum was no help. Chewing over these intriguing and unfathomable questions, Rosemary fell asleep.

* * *

Chapter Sixteen

Fortunately Hugo's declaration seemed to make no difference. The pattern of their lives went on as before.

Now the sunflowers were fully out, their dinner-plate heads turning the grey-green landscape gold.

Busy as she was with her painting and the simple domestic chores required of her, Rosemary couldn't get the mystery of the faded old postcard of St Julien le Grand out of her head.

And the pendulum was no help either.

No way could it cope with such questions as 'What connection does this small French village have with Mother ? With me ? With Aunt Mary ?' It was only after she'd worked out possible answers that the pendulum might tell her YES or NO.

A few nights after the trip to Bordeaux, pondering the mystery as usual as she drifted off to sleep, Rosemary suddenly came to a decision. She'd jolly well drive down there and investigate for herself. She should have thought of it earlier.

"I may not get back tonight," she explained to Hugo, packing her paints and easel into the car. "I thought I'd do a bit of exploring."

"OK," he said. "If you're not around by tomorrow evening I'll send out a search party. There's some wonderful country out towards Limoges. Turn right through the woods at the first roundabout . . ."

But she didn't. Rosemary knew exactly where she was going.

Without hesitation, she retraced the road they'd taken together, she and Hugo, the motorway south. She stopped again at Brantôme and had coffee in the same place as before. And then with mounting excitement, she drove on towards her goal.

WELCOME, said the sign, **TO ST JULIEN LE GRAND**.

With an inexplicable tingle, Rosemary pulled up on the tree-lined square. Having parked under a leafy oak, she made straight for the small shabby cafe where she ordered a Pernod and took it outside to the rickety trestle table covered in worn American cloth in faded green-and-yellow checks.

She'd brought the postcard with her, of course, and now she

took it out and again inspected the picture, a view of this very scene - the quiet tree-lined *place*, the shabby white-washed cottages, the squat church - and the cryptic message on the back : **'Remembering always'**.

The village hadn't changed much in the intervening years, that was for sure. There were a few cars parked in the picture now. TV aerials on most of the roofs. A lively supermarket on one corner where in the postcard she could see a pokey little bakery had stood. Otherwise . . .

"Can we join you ?"

A young couple came out of the café with glasses and sandwiches.

"That looks good," said Rosemary, and suddenly feeling peckish, she went in and ordered the same for herself.

"Are you touring these parts ?" the barman asked as he spooned black olives onto her plate alongside the hunk of crusty bread spread thickly with goats-milk cheese.

"I'm staying further north," she said. "Up on the Charente."

"Pretty country round there," he said. "In the sunflower belt, eh ?"

"Where I am, we're drowning in sunflowers."

"Civray ? I know Civray."

"Near there. It's at St Juste I'm staying . . ."

An elderly man who had been sitting with his back to them at a table in the window turned now.

"Ah," he said, coming over to the bar, "St Juste. St Juste sur Charente. That's familiar territory. My good wife came from those parts. I have a daughter near there."

Without needing to ask, the barman refilled his glass from the bottle of red wine on the counter, and gesturing to it, suggested Rosemary should try some herself. "The local vintage," he explained. "Nothing better."

"You're from England ?" the older man asked.

"Oh dear, is it so obvious ?"

"Actually, no. But I noticed the GB plates . . ."

"Trust you to spot that !" the barman said, wiping down the counter. "Jean-Marie is potty about England, the English . . ."

"I was over there in the war . . ."

"Were you ?"

101

"Will you sit here with me, my dear ?" he asked, indicating the table in the window. "It would be such a pleasure to indulge in a little English conversation."

His English was excellent.

"Jean-Marie Honoret is our local hero," said the barman, bringing the bottle over to their table. "Tell her about your adventures with the Free French, my friend."

"I'd rather you told me something about England, Madame. And about yourself," he said.

So she did, telling him about her painting, about the gîte among the sunflowers, about Betsy and . . . no, not Billy. That was too raw still, too painful.

"Betsy !" he said, interrupting. "That's a pretty name. I don't think we have a French equivalent, do we ?"

"It's not very common," she said. Betty, yes. But not Betsy. "It's a family name - we've dozens of Betsys. Across the generations."

He refilled their glasses and told her something of his life too. He was a blacksmith, he said, though he'd retired recently, passing the business on to his son.

"More than a blacksmith," the barman called over. "He's a bit of an artist, is Jean-Marie. Does all this fancy iron-work. Lamps, brackets, garden furniture - you know. Real fancy."

"Bruno exaggerates," said Jean-Marie modestly.

By the time she got up to leave, such warmth had developed between them that Rosemary heard herself inviting him to drop in on her in Mr Forêt's gîte next time he was visiting his daughter in Civray.

"I will do that," he said. "In fact, I was planning to drive up there in the next couple of weeks, so expect me shortly," and then with scarcely noticable hesitation, "chérie."

She had intended to explore the village, perhaps to paint it. But somehow, she had had her fill of St Julien le Grand. She had fulfilled her quest. Instead of pottering about in the afternoon's heat, Rosemary found she was quite ready to set off for home.

It was a long ride back. Putting on the headlights to pierce the gathering gloom, Rosemary twiddled with the radio and for the next thirty kilometres sang along heartily with the programme of operatic arias. La-la-la-ing when she didn't know the words :

102

"Funiculi funicula," sang the middle-aged English artist in her pale blue Morris Minor as she drove through deepest France in the sweet summer evening. "Funiculi funicula - la-la la-la. La-la lah."

It was pretty late when she arrived home. Hugo had left her a dish of thick cream in the fridge, and two of his wife's strawberry tarts. On the table was a note :

Visitors from England - Laurie and Prue.
I told them you'd probably be back tonight
so they hope to catch you in the morning.

Laurie. Laurie and Prue. What on earth could they be doing in France ? And how could they have tracked her down ? Betsy - of course. Betsy must have given them the address.

After a quick bath Rosemary carried a tray outside into the cool night and sat on the old stone bench in her cotton kaftan under Hugo's mulberry tree, under the new moon, to guzzle her strawberry tarts and cream. And to think back over her long and satisfying drive south. And the friends who were calling on her in the morning.

Climbing into bed, she was for once too tired to bother with the little wooden figures she was coming to identify so vividly, so appropriately, so mysteriously, with friends and family.

Tonight Rosemary fell instantly into a deep and dreamless sleep.

* * *

Chapter Seventeen

In spite of her long drive the day before, Rosemary was up bright and early.

"Ah, you are back then," said Hugo Forêt, finding her hanging the washing out when he and Erna arrived to milk the cows. "How far did you get ?"

"Actually, I simply retraced our route south. To take a good look round. It's such beautiful countryside . . ."

"I knew you would. It's that village, isn't it. That St Something le Grand ? Yes ?"

"Well, yes - I did find myself there again. Had lunch in this scruffy little bar . . ."

"You and your explorations ! So, did you discover anything there, anything to make the trip worth while ?"

"Of course not. It was a matter of simple curiosity. OK ? Now I can settle back into my painting routine."

"Huh !" said Hugo, looking sceptical. "I've a feeling there's something you're not telling me."

"Come on, now ! How about a cup of coffee ? I'm just fetching myself a refill."

Before he could answer, a camping van drew up at the gate, with a big rainbow painted along it.

"Rosie ! Hi ! You did get back then, Rosie !"

It was Laurie, of course. But a very different Laurie from the one she'd been expecting. He was bearded and dressed in wacky Eastern gear - a yellow kaftan, Jesus sandals - with his grey hair tied back in a pigtail, and strings of beads and shells and feathers round his neck.

"Laurie, love," she said, going over to open the gate. "What a nice surprise ! And this must be Prue."

The young woman was a good six inches taller than him, with a tumble of Titian curls. And in spite of being hugely pregnant she was sporting equally colourful gear, a pink and silver sari dotted with tiny mirrors that caught the light and shimmered. Laurie and Prue were clearly exotic New Age travellers. And with a vengeance.

"Come in, come in."

They were both enchanted by the farmyard, the ancient barn with its store of neatly stacked logs, the mulberry tree, the panoramic view across the valley of the Charente.

"How on earth did you find me ?"

"Betsy gave us instructions. I was fortunate to catch her. She'd only just got back from London."

"We parked down there beside the river," said Prue. "It was a heavenly camp site."

"I'd got a hunch that you'd be back," said Laurie. "We were beaming out love and light, weren't we Prue ? To bring you home. It always works."

Rosemary showed them round the farmhouse with as much pride as if it had been her own.

"Goodness, you've been busy !" Laurie said when he saw the paintings propped up around the sittingroom. "I'd forgotten how talented you are."

"How long is it since we last met, Laurie ?" she asked as they gathered under the mulberry tree with their fresh coffee. "How long have you two been together ? I've lost track."

"Three years," said Prue shyly.

"I'm a lucky man."

"You look well on it, both of you."

And it was true, they both looked radiantly happy.

It could so easily have been me with Laurie, Rosemary thought. Sharing his New Age quests. He'd asked her often enough. Begged her even. To leave Pete and move over to Ireland with him.

"You'd love it," he'd said. "You'd all love it."

Yes, she remembered that he'd been prepared to take them on board as a family - Billy and Betsy and all. Thank god she'd avoided that pitfall.

Thank god for Prudence !

"How did you and Laurie meet ?" Prue asked Rosemary.

They'd met in London several years before.

"Janet and Sue are going up to Olympia," she'd told Pete. "To this New Age-y do." The Festival of Mind, Body and Spirit.

"What gullible fools they must be."

"And I've decided to go with them. Right. Saturday. We're setting out good and early . . ."

105

"Hang on. What about us ?"

"The kids will be no trouble. Betsy's got her ballet - Sarah's mother will collect her. I'll do the shopping on Friday and leave you a casserole for supper."

"It's all right for some, eh. Can't remember when I last had a trip to town."

"There's nothing to stop you going up, Pete." He could jump on a train any time. School holidays, Saturdays. Any time. He held the purse strings, after all.

"I didn't think I'd be able to get away," Rosemary told the others as they drew into the first Happy Eater to treat themselves to a motorway breakfast. "Pete can't stand being left in charge."

"Neither can Mike."

"None of them can."

The Festival was staggering.

There were stalls selling herbs, psychedelic posters and badges, incense, tarot cards, mystical tapes, chunks of healing crystal . . .

"Look here," said Janet, reading from a blackboard. "Agate for fevers, jade for the kidneys, amethyst to protect against diseases of the blood . . ."

"Could put us all out of work," said Sue. They were both nurses.

"Onyx for deafness, lepidolite for the heart . . ."

"But not for broken hearts."

"There's no cure for broken hearts." After twenty-three years, Janet's marriage had just fallen apart.

There were books on witchcraft, the I Ching and holistic diets. And in a corridor of colourful booths were the Fortune Tellers : Tarot Readers, Clairvoyants and Palmists, practitioners of aromatherapy and psychometry.

At the Dianetics stall, they each took a free Personality Test but managed to resist the efforts of the team of shiny-eyed Americans who were determined to sell them a copy of their bible, a hefty tome by Ron L Hubbard, humanist and philosopher. And millionaire.

"I can see you are well on the path to spiritual enlightenment," one young evangelist said, offering Rosemary a copy. "I'll let you have it for £10."

"Let's have a look," said Sue, thumbing quickly through it. "Ah, I like

106

this - Question 189 : Are you able to resist high pressure selling ?"

"'Fraid we are, darling," Janet said, plonking the sacred text back on the pile. And they waltzed off laughing.

They had their auras painted by a pale waif, and sat cross-legged on the floor to share in a meditation.

"I'm going to treat myself to some rune stones," Janet said. "Look at that set." The runic symbols were etched into a collection of small smooth pebbles. "Oh, yes please."

They all had their palms read, and Kirlian photographs of their hands taken, all radiating rainbows.

"I must keep an eye on the time," Sue said as they perched on the wall beside the fountain with cans of coke. Knowing the ropes from previous visits, the first thing she had done when they arrived was book a tarot reading. For mid-day.

"Hey ! Look at that !"

Regression under Hypnosis, the banner said. **Discover your past lives**.

"Do we need to book a time ?" Janet asked.

"I can do you at mid-day," the elderly hypnotist told her. "Bring a tape and we can record your experiences of times past. Right."

"I'll sit here," Rosemary said, settling herself at a table in the Zodiac Snack Bar while the others went off to their appointments. She'd flick through the collection of colourful brochures and leaflets they'd picked up as they went round the stalls. She was quite ready for a sit down and a cup of herbal tea, and it would be good to watch this exotic world go by from her quiet corner.

"Do you mind if I join you ?" asked the short trim man standing awkwardly there with a tray of healthy looking lunch.

"Please do." And Rosemary gathered up the reading matter which she'd strewn all over the table.

"The name's Laurie . . ."

He was a flyer, it turned out. An Aer Lingus pilot.

"I had a few hours to spare between flights," he told her. "I've always been fascinated by all this Paranormal stuff."

By the time Janet and Sue came back from their psychic sessions, Laurie and Rosemary had discovered a good deal about each other.

"It was all so vivid, so incredibly familiar," Janet told them, stunned by her session with the hypnotist who had apparently managed to take her back to a past life in what she described as a Stone Age settlement. "I mean, I knew the people, I recognised them all. I could have named every one of them : Lod, Bork, Seti, Larsh - it was uncanny."

"Did you get it on tape, then ?"

"I did. We could listen to it on the way home."

"Oh, my stars," Laurie said, looking at his watch, "it's time I was going. Mustn't be late back. They'll be wondering what I've been up to, my crew. I wouldn't mind being regressed myself. Still, duty calls. I've so enjoyed meeting you all." As he left he offered Rosemary his card, "Just in case any of you should ever find yourself at a loose end in Dublin," he said with an apologetic grin.

She hadn't gone to Dublin, but having exchanged Christmas cards, a couple of letters and two or three phone calls, Laurie had invited Rosemary up to London again.

"How about this year's Mind, Body and Spirit thing ?" he'd asked, phoning her on a school day when he knew she'd be on her own.

"When is it ? I hadn't thought about it ?"

"All this week. I'm free tomorrow, my rest day. Wondered if you could get up on the train. I could meet you at Waterloo . . ."

And that was it. She was still very much married, and full of guilt at betraying Pete, even to this extent - an innocent rendez-vous at a New Age fair.

"That hypnotist is here again. Shall we see whether he can regress us ?"

"Do let's. Janet's experience was totally amazing. In fact it's changed her life. She's training to be a healer, a foot healer, what do they call it ?"

"Reflexology."

"Yes. A reflexologist. She's gone all spiritual."

"Can we sit in on one another's sessions ?" Laurie asked the hypnotist.

"No problem."

Rosemary went first.

"It seemed somehow Medieval," she told Laurie afterwards. "And it was so darned vivid."

Mr Proudfoot had no crystal pendulum for her to fix her eyes on. There was no hocus-pocus at all. Once Rosemary was comfortable on his sofa, he asked her to concentrate on the softness of the cushions at her back, the weight of her arm on her lap, the heaviness of her eyelids on her closed eyes.

"Now we're putting your conscious mind on Hold," he said, "and together we are switching into your subconscious."

That was all straightforward enough.

"Right, now when I count to three, I'm going to tap your forehead and take you back and back and back . . ."

It was as easy as that.

"Where are you ?" he asked Rosemary.

I'm still here with you, she wanted to tell him. I can still hear all the activity out there, the music, the chatter. I can still feel your arm against mine.

And yet, even as she thought this, she found herself drifting away. Away from HERE and NOW, away to THERE and THEN. To begin with she seemed to be suspended in limbo, floating in the swirling mists of time.

"The way you feel when you are rudely awoken from deep sleep," she was to tell Laurie afterwards. "By the baby crying . . ."

"Yes, or the phone ringing - the struggle it is to surface, to drag yourself awake. I felt the same."

"Tell you what it reminded me of," she said, as he saw her onto her train that evening, "it was a bit like looking through an old album of family photos and seeing myself as a baby, right. There's not the slightest resemblance between the woman I am today and that baby in the heavy old pram being pushed along a Somerset lane. And yet I know for certain that it is me, this blonde beaming baby. I can't remember the day or the circumstances in which it was taken, but I know without a doubt that it is a photo of me. It was a similar feeling."

She had found herself in a high meadow with woods below her, the sweet smell of new mown hay, and in the distance her home - a one-roomed cottage, a hovel really, with dry-stone walls and a shabby thatched roof. Her possessions were few. For a table there was a rough board balanced on piles of stone at which she now found she was making bread. There was a low wooden bedstead with what she knew to be a pine-needle palliasse. Beside the hearth there was a basket with a baby in it.

"I was Mathilda," she told Laurie. She *was* this other woman, and at the same time she was observing her. "My man was Arthur. I could see it all. I could smell the fresh-baked loaves cooling at the door. More than that, it was familiar territory. I recognised it all"

"I hoped your man would have turned out to have been a Medieval Laurie," he said, with his shy grin.

Going over it again in the train home, Rosemary remembered how now and again the hypnotist had nudged her with a question such as, "Is there any one else there with you ?" And yes, there were others with her. Several others.

Here again, it was like a photo. An old school photo, say, that you haven't taken out of the drawer for years. Row upon row of lumpy girls in gym-slips, right. You know them all, just about, but you can't for the life of you put a name to any except those few special friends.

That's how it was under Mr Proudfoot's hypnotic spell, she thought. When he asked, "What is her name ?" or "What do you call him ?" she hadn't been able to answer straight away. It took a great effort to bring the name back out of the darkness.

"Hope you're not going to get embroiled in all this New Age nonsense," Pete said, when she got back. "I have my reputation to think of."

It was then that Rosemary had decided she must break away from Pete. There was nothing left between them. Nothing but cold resentment. The very next morning she found a solicitor and set the divorce proceedings in motion. Funny that. And on such slender provocation.

"I can't understand you," Pete was to say when she moved into the spare room and he began to realise she was serious. "We get along OK don't we - no worse than most. I've done my best."

"We've each done our best." She'd come to feel that in the bleakness of their marriage the life was being squeezed out of her. As if she was being slowly throttled. Garrotted.

"I'll try to change," he said. "I somehow hadn't realised that you were unhappy." And awkwardly, shyly her husband buried his face in her hair and wept. "We could go back and start again."

But it was too late for that. There was no going back - there was nothing to go back to. It had been threadbare from the start.

But she and Laurie had found a way back.

"Do you remember how we were regressed, both of us ?" she asked him now under Hugo Forêt's mulberry tree.

"That really changed me, the regression," he said. "Changed the whole direction of my life."

Rosemary knew this was true. Shortly afterwards, he'd written to tell her he had taken early retirement. Then there had been regular phone calls, and letters - first warm, then affectionate and before long passionate.

"Come over to Ireland, Rosemary. Come and see how it could be for us together here. Do come . . ."

But she hadn't. Fond as she had become of Laurie, she knew it would have been a mistake. She used the children as her excuse.

"They don't want to be uprooted. Billy's got his A's coming up. Betsy's just starting at the Big School. They've got their friends. There's been enough of an upheaval as it is . . ." The divorce was proving traumatic for all of them.

"And it changed mine too," said Prue, giving him a secret smile. They glowed with happiness, the pair of them.

Following the regression, Laurie had found himself drawn into a variety of New Age groups, he told Rosemary. Before long, he'd met Prue who was one of a team of healers living together in a dilapidated mansion in the Forest of Dean. Her thing was colour - colour therapy. Using rainbow ribbons and coloured lights, she seemed to be able to help people to overcome grief and guilt and despair. And through the specialised use of colour in their clothes and their environment, help them back to health and happiness.

"I was completely amazed at the work Prue was doing, at her incredible gift . . ."

"Oh, rubbish," Prue protested. "It's only a matter of studying the masters."

"I soon got drawn into the community . . ."

"He's doing a homoeopathy course at Bristol . . ."

"We're on our way to a Mid-Summer Camp . . ."

"A gathering of mystics and healers and whatnot . . ."

"Near Biarritz."

"You could come with us, Rosemary. Share our van."

But she didn't.

Rosemary had found a few hours with these two quite enough, thank you.

"They are a really sweet pair," she explained to Hugo after they'd gone. Such loving, gentle, positive souls, eager to see the best in people. "But I seem to have grown out of all that New Age stuff."

Quite worn out by Laurie and Prue and their enthusiasms, Rosemary found she was ready for bed immediately after supper, but it was a mistake - she was too tired to sleep.

I must be getting old, she thought. Never mind, New Age - I feel decidedly middle-aged tonight.

After tossing about for a while, she gave up and got out of bed to lean out of the window enjoying the cool night air and the scent of the honeysuckle growing up the wall.

Back in bed, Rosemary took down Aunt Mary's brick-box. It may have been the moonlight that deceived her, but she suddenly realised that among the little wooden figures spread out on the quilt was one that she hadn't noticed before, one that looked incredibly like Laurie, but the old Laurie as she'd first known him, smart, slim, dapper and conventional. Only in the intense brown of his eyes was there a hint of what he might become - the fervent hippie, with the loose yellow smock, the beard, the pigtail, the carved beads around his neck. But still her dear old Laurie.

How extraordinary !

* * *

Chapter Eighteen

A week later Rosemary had another visitor. As she tidied up the kitchen before setting off for a day's painting, she heard a car draw up outside the farm gate, and next minute there was the tall thin bearded figure of Jean-Marie Honoret at the door.

"As you're not on the phone," he said, "I decided I'd drop by."

"Oh, what a lovely surprise. Come in."

"You were just going out," he said, noticing her paints and rucksack and easel standing ready.

"It doesn't matter. Sit down and I'll make some coffee."

Again, she recognised this feeling he somehow produced in her. A comfortableness, a contentment.   Alongside a buzz of expectation. Although they'd only spent an hour or so together before in the bar in St Julien, here they were chatting like old friends.

"Now you must tell me something about your war," she said, sitting him down at the table with his coffee. "About your time in England."

"One day I will," he said. "But not today. My daughter is expecting me shortly. I mustn't be long."

"It's funny having visitors. Over here." And she told him about Laurie and Prue. "First them and now you - I'm beginning to feel as if I live here."

"Perhaps you were meant to," he said. "Perhaps it's in your blood."

"Or in my stars !" she said. "They were deeply into all that New Age stuff, those two - astrology, tarot, colour psychology. That was Prue. She's years younger than him . . ."

"Age doesn't matter, does it ?"

No, she thought. No, it doesn't matter at all.

"I'd not met her before."

When I met him, she thought, Laurie was very different. Buttoned-up, sad, lonely. "Although we've lost touch, for several years he was a big influence on me."

"Oh, yes !" said Jean-Marie with a knowing look.

"No, no - it wasn't like that at all. He made me realise that I didn't have to stay married. That escape was possible."

"It's all very well for you people. Protestants. Marriage over here still means for life."

He'd not said anything about his wife, his marriage. Rosemary had assumed he was a widower.

"Yes, I've a great deal to thank him for. Laurie." Apart from the kids, she had come to feel her life had only really started after the divorce. With Pete it was a half-life. If that. Until Laurie put the idea in her head, she had somehow assumed that there was no alternative. "Now it's like a dream," she told Jean-Marie. "All those years of marriage - a bad dream."

"Funnily enough, I dreamt about you last night," he told her. "Well, no - not about you, but about someone I used to know. A lifetime ago." And standing back from her as if judging a picture, a portrait, he said, "You remind me of her."

Suddenly shy with him, Rosemary changed the subject.

"Laurie was telling me about these dreams he used to have. He's a pilot, right. Or he was. He said that half-a-dozen times over the years he's had a dream which later, within a week or so, came true . . ."

"I hope my dream, last night's dream comes true."

She didn't hear him. Or chose not to. Not yet.

"In these dreams of mine," Laurie had told Rosemary and Prue and Hugo as they sat out on the stone bench with glasses of red wine before the travellers set off for Biarritz, "in each of them I had a vivid premonition of an air crash."

For twenty years Laurie had served in the RAF, first as a pilot, later as a flying instructor.

"I had been trained to observe, assess and record events. Objectively and accurately."

The first of these dreams had come to him when he was a young pilot.

"I was in a Lincoln," he told them, "not flying it myself but observing from behind the pilot's seat, as it were. I knew in my dream that I knew the crew, knew them but somehow couldn't put a name to either of them. The aircraft was coming in to land at an airfield I recognised. Hemswell it was, RAF Hemswell . . ."

"My father came from Hemswell," said Prue.

"Right," he said, putting a loving arm around her shoulders. "As the aircraft touched down it bounced and to my horror the pilot opened up the engines to go round again, something you couldn't do in a Lincoln."

In his dream, the aircraft had swung out of control. Too late the pilot had realised his mistake - the plane crashed on the field.

"By now," Laurie said, "it was as if I was seeing the scene from some fifty feet above the plane, above the Runway Controller's cabin. I saw the crew get out and run from the wreck before it burst into flames. And then I awoke."

"And . . . ?" The others were spell-bound.

"And some ten days later there was a crash at RAF Hemswell. It happened exactly as I'd seen in my dream. It turned out that the pilot had been with me through Flying School and afterwards at the Advanced Flying Unit at Wellington but we had lost touch since then. It was very odd, very worrying."

The other premonitions had all involved flying accidents and in each case the pilot was a friend of Laurie's. And apart from the Hemswell incident, in each case the pilot was killed in the crash.

"Did you tell anybody ?" Rosemary asked him. "About the dreams ?"

"I didn't. And even now I've only told Prue and the people at Cinderford. And you two," he had said, embracing Rosemary and shaking Hugo's hand warmly, before the pair of them climbed into their rainbow van. "Flyers are very superstitious. If word had got around, I would have been ostracised - no-one would have risked flying with me."

"We heard some pretty strange stories of that sort during the war," said Jean-Marie Honoret now. "It really made you wonder. About ghosts and psychic warnings and telepathy and things."

"Perhaps there *are* more things in heaven and earth . . ."

"Who knows," he said. "But one thing's for sure - I must be on my way. I can see you're itching to get out there among the sunflowers. And my daughter's expecting me for lunch. May I call again ? In a week or two ?"

"Of course. Of course. Even if I'm not in, Hugo will be around the farmyard and he'll know where I am, more or less."

She walked out to the gate with him.

"My stars !" she said, seeing his battered old black Citroen. "It's a wonder you made it."

"My most faithful friend, my Deuche," he said, patting it affectionately on the bonnet. "It'll see me out, I suspect."

"Goodbye Jean-Marie - see you again soon."

"A bientôt, chérie." And he was gone.

After this, Jean-Marie took to calling on Rosemary whenever he came up to visit his daughter in Civray.

"That old fellow here again this morning !" muttered Hugo stocking her up with logs. "What's he up to, eh ?"

"Up to ? He pops in on his way to see his daughter."

"She's a friend of ours, his Louisa. A neighbour in fact. She's getting quite suspicious about it. They used to see him once a year. If they were lucky. At Christmas, say. But now . . . this is his third visit in so many weeks."

"Don't ask me."

But she had her suspicions too.

* * *

Chapter Nineteen

Now in high summer, it was too hot to paint all day. And with the heat came the thunderstorms. As often as not, in the early afternoon the sky would darken and the heavens open.

Rosemary began to get up earlier, as soon as it was light, and set off with her painting gear immediately after breakfast. She'd usually left before Hugo turned up to see to the farm stock.

She had found a spot beside the river from where she could see the red roofs of the town, the golden fields of sunflowers glowing gloriously against the delicate green of the birch trees. She'd painted this scene several times, in different lights and different moods.

This morning she was interrupted in her work.

"Eh bien," said the elegantly-dressed woman who stopped to peer at Rosemary's canvas. "They said I'd find you here."

"I love this spot - I often come here." It was true. she did love it. The richness of the colours, the babbling of the river, the tranquillity.

"You are from England, yes ?"

"Yes. Though I seem to have settled in here. I should be going back home."

"Yes, it is time you left."

"Excuse me ?"

Astonished at the woman's aggressive tone, Rosemary put her brush down and steeled herself for battle. Was this perhaps Hugo's wife, Mme Forêt ? Could she have fathomed out her husband's feelings for the visitor from England, the tenant of the farmhouse ? Had she heard that Rosemary had gone with him on the trip to Bordeaux ?

"You don't know who I am, then ?" the woman asked.

"I'm afraid I don't."

"I'm Louisa, Louisa Prades. Jean-Marie Honoret is my father."

"Ah !" said Rosemary, beginning to understand. "I'm pleased to meet you."

"Well, we're not too happy about you. You and Papa. What are you up to, Madame ?"

"Up to ? Why, nothing. What can you mean ? He has called in on me a couple of times, it's true. I suspect he enjoys the chance to talk English. And he seems to be interested in my work . . ."

"Please - I'm not daft. It's a hell of drive for him - well over a hundred kilometres, three hours and more. And suddenly he's coming up here every week or so. What's going on, Madame ? My mother fears the worst."

"Oh, come on - Jean-Marie, er - your father is twenty years older than me. At least. What are you suggesting ?"

"I'm just warning you. Watch your step, Madame. Mother nearly lost him to an English woman. Years ago. It's time you returned home, Rosemary Richardson. You have done more than enough mischief already."

And stiff with moral indignation, Louisa Prades went on her way.

He has a wife then, thought Rosemary. Though there's nothing for me to be feeling guilty about. The most he had ever done was kiss her politely - kiss-kiss-kiss, left-right-left - in greeting. And give her a bear hug when he left.

And yet . . .

And yet there was something smouldering between them. Something powerful. Unlike anything she had ever felt before. There was sex in it, yes. But there was more to it than that, something primitive and magnetic. What was it that was developing between herself and this elderly Frenchman, Jean-Marie Honoret ?

The sky suddenly darkened, a signal for Rosemary to gather up her paints and dash for home before the storm started.

It was the very next day that Jean-Marie turned up again. Unexpected as usual. Unannounced. But this time it was mid-afternoon when he arrived, in the middle of the storm.

"Hello !" she said, suddenly awkward with him. "I was just going to make a pot of tea."

"I've come up specially. Louisa phoned me . . ."

"What an outburst !" she said. "I'd no idea that I was causing all this trouble."

"I was afraid she'd frighten you off, that you'd have packed up and gone."

"No, no - it would take more than that to scare me away."

118

"I think I owe you an explanation," he said.

She had already lit the fire and as it was burning merrily they took their chairs over and the tea and settled down beside it.

"I am married," he said. "Elize is in hospital, poor soul. In a home for the disabled, the Hospital of the Holy Virgin. Up here in Civray, right. It's MS - Multiple Sclerosis. She's been ill for years. Because she was local born and bred, the nuns agreed to take her in when we could no longer cope at home. And Louisa being up here as well . . . She's completely helpless now. They are very good, very kind, the Little Sisters of Charity. When I come up here, I visit her and my daughter. And nowadays, you too."

"I'm so sorry," Rosemary said.

"From what Louisa said, I was afraid she'd spoilt everything between us. Afraid she'd sullied our friendship."

"No. No fear of that, love." Rosemary reached over and stroked his strong gnarled blacksmith's hand, and then quickly, for fear she was overstepping some invisible line, she took his cup to refill it, as if the intimacy had been accidental.

"Years ago," he began, "during the war something happened. In England. Later, foolishly, I told Elize about it. She never forgave me. Louisa reckoned it had triggered off her illness, the shock it gave her. I knew this was impossible, but it's left me feeling guilty, responsible, a big disappointment."

"But what's that got to do with me ? Now ?" Rosemary asked. Amazed.

"They're inclined to look on me as a womaniser, an adulterer. And they are both fiercely religious which has made everything worse."

"Tell me about your war ? Your time in England."

"It's a long story . . ."

He'd only been a lad when the war started.

"With my brother Charles and another chap, Raoul, we attempted to get across to England to join up with an undercover unit we'd heard was operating from Weymouth."

"The Free French ?" Rosemary asked.

Jean-Marie laughed. "I don't know. I didn't even know if there **was** such a unit. I was seventeen, my dear, and my head was filled with adventures and heroics."

But things had gone wrong. Their small craft - a fishing boat requisitioned from a group in St Nazaire - ran into a frightful storm.

"It was a miracle we didn't capsize . . ."

They were blown way off course and were eventually washed up on a rocky beach on the Scilly Isles.

"Raoul, poor soul, was bashed on the rocks and drowned."

Jean-Marie sat silent, staring into the flames, remembering his comrades and that distant darkness.

Leaving him for a moment, Rosemary went to get the bottle of brandy from the sideboard.

"And you . . . ? You and your brother ?"

"We were fortunate . . ."

Although it was dead of night when their boat was flung onto the rocks, help arrived almost at once.

"There was a constant watch around the islands - with Jersey in enemy hands, fear of invasion was strong."

Having searched them for weapons, Jean-Marie and his brother were taken off to be interrogated.

"Once they were satisfied with our story," he told her now, "we were advised to join the Free French. The best they could do was to take us across to Cornwall and then . . ."

They still wanted to join this special unit, so once ashore, they passed from one fishing community to another, along the North Cornwall coast, always pretending that they were on their way to join the main Free French force. Clothed and fed along the way, travelling under cover of darkness, the brothers eventually found themselves in Clevedon.

"At this point we decided to separate. It seemed safer to travel alone. Less likely to arouse suspicion."

He had found his way to the station and managed to creep into a goods wagon and bury himself in the straw packing around some wooden crates. First stop Bristol.

"At Temple Meads I stowed away on the late night train to Weymouth. I hid in the WC and once we were on our way slipped out and found a seat."

After an hour or so, he'd heard a bit of a commotion further along the train. Shouts, protests.

"I thought it was the police. Perhaps the Military Police. I'm afraid I panicked."

As casually as possible, he'd left his seat as if to visit the loo.

Just then the train happened to be slowing down slightly as it started up a steep incline.

"I jumped," Jean-Marie told her. "I opened the door and jumped."

"Jumped !" He could have been killed.

There was a knock on the door and without waiting for an invitation, Hugo came in, dripping wet from the storm.

"Oh - excusez-moi. I didn't know you had a visitor, again," he said pointedly, though he must have seen the car at the gate. "The electricity seems to have failed. Could be the storm, could be the generator. Can I check your supply, Marie-Rose ?"

"If the storm's easing off, I'll be on my way," said Jean-Marie, sensing disapproval.

"But then what ? You haven't finished the story."

"Another time," he said. "Another time." And he left.

Hugo Forêt looked far from friendly when he came back from testing the lights. If one was working, he'd have known they all were, Rosemary thought, but let it pass.

"What's that old fool playing at ?" he demanded fiercely, no doubt recalling his own recent declaration and rejection.

"Come on ! He's not that old . . ."

"Folk are beginning to talk, you know. They could make it very unpleasant for you. There's nothing these religious types like more than a good old scandal. Beware, Marie-Rose. You can pop back to England, but he'd be stuck with it."

"But there's nothing for anyone to get upset about, there's nothing going on, I promise you."

"Don't be so naive, chérie - it's enough that they think there's something. We are very old-fashioned in these parts, and the Church still has a powerful grip on everyone."

Maybe they are right, Rosemary thought, lying awake that night as the last of the thunder rumbled around the sunflower fields. Maybe it is time I went home.

Next day she went into Civray to check ferry sailings without actually booking one. She popped into the Coq d'Or for a coffee.

"We haven't seen you for a week or two," Anton said, with no hint of antagonism. "Do come and eat with us tonight, Rosemary. Our Fortune Teller will be here - Lucille le Farge - remember ? And Pierre is going to town on the desserts. Please come."

"I'd love to," she said. "Thank you."

"And your pictures are selling a treat - I'll have a cheque ready for you this evening. We could hang a few more if you have some ready."

"Oh, great ! How many ? Another half-dozen or so ?"

"Easily."

"Bless you, Anton - I should take you on as my agent."

"Be here for seven-thirty - OK ?"

Rosemary had one or two chores to do in the town - at the post office, the bank, the bakery. And for the first time, in all these minor transactions she could feel antagonism. Suspicion. Disapproval.

Before she'd finished, the storm broke. By the time she got back to the car she was drenched and miserable.

Back home, Rosemary towelled her hair and with a strong childish need for warmth and security, filled her hot water bottle and went upstairs. Stripping off her wet clothes she crawled into the Forêt family's enormous old bed and burying herself in the vast feather duvet she cried herself to sleep.

* * *

Chapter Twenty

"Now then," said Anton when the coffee was served, "what have you got for us tonight, Lucille ?"

There were a dozen of them gathered round the big table under the window in Le Coq d'Or. Eight of them had eaten together, the others, at the prospect of a little of Lucille's magic, trickling in from the tables outside.

"Tonight we will see what the tarot cards have to tell us," said Lucille who was wearing the most gorgeous dress of dark red velvet, with pearls in her ears and in her hair.

"Take care," someone said. "Father Dominique is eating outside with the Fabriquant family."

"He's gone," said someone else, checking at the door.

"Some people would be only too ready to report us to the priests," Anton whispered to Rosemary. "The Tarot is supposed to be the Devil's Picture Book."

While she shuffled the tarot cards, one of Lucille's young acolytes kept an eye on the door.

"Uh-hu !" There was a late-comer.

It was Hugo Forêt. "I couldn't get away earlier," he explained. "Sorry."

"Right," she said, when everyone was ready, all sitting round expectantly. "Because there are so many of us here, we could either do one serious reading which might take an hour or more, or we can do mini readings for everyone . . ."

"Yes, yes," they said, all wanting a go, no matter how sceptical they might say they were. "Mini readings all round."

One-by-one, going round the table anti-clockwise - "Widdershins, to assist the magic." - Lucille invited each of them to first shuffle the pack of cards, and then cut it into three and pick up the top card from each pile, three cards each, and hand them to her to analyse.

"Oh, Anton," she told him seriously, "this Knight of Pentacles is bad news and shows you are always attracted to beautiful people, young and beautiful but nowhere near your equal intellectually. This probably means the relationships will hardly ever last. In spite of their youth and good looks, you will soon become bored . . ."

There was much laughter at this. Anton's homosexuality was no secret. Young Pierre was not at the table. Having helped clear the dishes away, he'd chosen to go and watch a video upstairs.

Creating a mixture of laughter and tears, Lucille read on around the table.

"Ah - the Magician. Beware of a very persuasive talker, a manipulator . . ."

"The Three of Cups is the card that promises rejoicing. Soon those who love you, who care about you, will have reason to rejoice on your behalf. Maybe there's good news coming to you. Of a success, an opportunity, a contract, a baby - but whatever it is, it will bring you and others a great deal of happiness . . ."

"The Eight of Swords is very painful. It tells me that you are feeling trapped, imprisoned, hopeless. But do not despair - there is a way out of your predicament . . ."

And now it was Hugo's turn.

"This is interesting," Lucille said. "The Five of Cups is the card of disappointment, symbolising feelings of waste and pointlessness, repressed dreams. The High Priestess is a very powerful symbol of intuition and psychic understanding. In this spread her power is negative which probably means you are under pressure from a strong-willed woman who has appropriated the authority of the church, her church, to control you. The Eight of Pentacles gives you an answer though it may not be the answer you were hoping for. It tells you to accept the situation you are in, forget the dreams, concentrate on your work, and happiness will be yours, the happiness that comes from pride in your strength and skill and in your ability to control and master your desires."

"Poor old Hugo," someone said. "That's not much consolation."

They'd all drunk a fair amount by now - wine, coffee, cognac. By the time Lucille reached Rosemary the party had become noisy and tipsy.

"Ah-ha," someone said, with a knowing grin, "Hugo's English artist . . ."

"This should be good."

Rosemary's cards were all trumps.

"The tarot trumps are the powerful and mysterious archetypes which have fascinated philosophers and mystics for centuries,"

Lucille explained. "T.S.Eliot, Jung, Einstein - all kinds of distinguished thinkers have studied the tarot trumps. Their origin is lost in the mist of time."

"Never mind all that bull-shit . . ."

"Fill up her glass, François."

At last they settled down to hear what the cards had to say to the stranger in their midst, this independent (dangerously independent) artist from across the Channel.

Rosemary's cards were these : the Moon, the Emperor, and the Fool.

"No need to snigger at the Fool," Lucille told them. "The Fool is quite the most beautiful of all the cards. You'll see."

She told Rosemary that the Moon stood for a journey of sorrow and pain and self-loathing. The Emperor stood for male-ness. Particularly fatherhood. The Fool symbolised optimism and liberation.

"It seems to me that all your life you have suffered serious abuse at the hands of men, possibly at the hands of your father. Or your supposed father," Lucille added mysteriously. "From these cards, especially from the position of the Emperor" (which was standing on his head in front of Rosemary), "I'd say that some surprising information is coming to you which will turn your early sufferings upside down. The guilt and disgust which you have felt about certain aspects of your life, your childhood, will be wiped away, leaving you free to dance into the future, no longer burdened by the past."

Rosemary was deeply shaken by this interpretation of her three cards. Thinking of Father and his disgusting games, the power that she had allowed men to wield over her, one after the other : Father, Fred Sixsmith, Pete, Edward. Why had she been so weak and silly ?

This was quite the most serious reading Lucille had given so far. Hugo - bless him - moved quietly round to stand behind her with his hands protectively on the back of her chair. Anton brought her some fresh-made coffee, extra strong and laced with cognac. Somehow Rosemary controlled her tears. Fortunately by this time most of the party were too merry to take much in.

As soon as she decently could, Rosemary got up to leave.

"That was terribly interesting," she said to Lucille shaking her hand. "Do we owe you anything for our readings ?"

"No, no," the Tarot Reader said, coming round the table to embrace her. "These are very superficial analyses, just giving you a taste of the tarot. I charge for a full reading, of course, but that takes a good hour and must be undertaken in quiet and privacy."

"I think I'd like a serious reading," Rosemary said. "Perhaps you'd come up to the farmhouse one day ?"

"I'd like to do that. Hugo will let me know when you feel ready - yes ?"

"Goodnight. Goodnight, Anton - it was a splendid meal, a splendid evening. Goodnight all."

Hugo followed her out to the car, putting an arm round her shoulders as they crossed the cobbles.

"Are you OK ?" he asked. "I could see that the reading shook you - do you want me to drive you home ? The bike's in the barn so I can be back in no time."

But she didn't - she longed to be alone. To take a long clear look at her life.

As so often before, when she was in bed Rosemary took down Aunt Mary's box of nine-pins and spread the little wooden figures around her on the quilt.

Yes, it was time to take stock.

Somehow the likenesses between the carved figures and all these characters in her life seemed stronger than ever tonight, but perhaps that was due to Anton's generosity with the wine and the cognac.

She sorted the figures into teams. Into a plus pile and a minus pile.

Into the negative pile went the Father figure, and Fred Sixsmith, and Pete, and - yes, painful as it was to admit it - her lovely Edward.

Into the other group she put Laurie, dear harmless Laurie. And Billy of course. And on reflection, the Hugo Forêt mannikin too. He was proving a stalwart friend in spite of her rejection.

There were two figures left. Unaccounted for. But hang on. This one - tall, thin, elderly and bearded - this one was the spitting image of Jean-Marie. Oh, heavens, yes ! Why hadn't she seen it before, the incredible likeness.

To be honest, Rosemary was no longer surprised at the extraordinary way in which the skittles were tying in with the significant men in her own life. She'd grown accustomed to the magic.

Before putting them back in their box, she had another look at the sepia postcard, half-hoping that having found St Julien Le Grand and visited it, she would somehow be able to decipher its significance. But no, the card and its message were quite as mysterious now as they'd ever been. She must ask Jean-Marie about it. Next time he called.

Yes, of course - why hadn't she thought of it earlier.

* * *

Chapter Twenty-One

It was nearly a fortnight before Jean-Marie next called.

I guess Louisa has been on at him again, Rosemary thought bleakly.

But when at last he came to the door, everything seemed fine between them.

"I thought I'd best keep away," he said, giving her an extra powerful bear hug. "Give them a chance to cool down."

"Have you time for a drink, Jean-Marie? Coffee? Tea? Something stronger?"

It was a hot morning. Too hot to sit comfortably outside. With a pleasant draught from the open door, the kitchen was wonderfully cool.

"You didn't finish your story . . ." Rosemary reminded him as she poured the coffee.

"I don't want to bore you . . ."

"Bore me! You'd just jumped from the moving train, for Christ's sake!"

"Fancy you remembering!"

Fortunately, he had happened to jump at a spot where the train slowed down, where the track started up a steep incline, above a grassy embankment . . .

"There was a railway embankment at the back of Aunt Mary's cottage," Rosemary suddenly remembered. "When we were kids, the steam trains used to be chuffing up and down all day."

Between Taunton and Yeovil. Bristol and the South Coast. Thanks to Dr Beeching it had been closed years ago. The lines had been taken up, the sleepers. You could still walk along the old trackway - it had gradually turned into a wild-life haven.

Jean-Marie had more or less rolled down the railway embankment, landing in a tangle of brambles and nettles.

"And I'd done my ankle in. Fractured a bone, it turned out. Aargh - it was excruciating," and his face screwed up in remembered agony. "I had to lie still for a while trying not to scream."

Eventually he'd managed to crawl through the undergrowth.

"And bless me, there was a shed," he told Rosemary, "there among the apple trees was a small tumble-down shed."

He'd dragged himself inside it and curled up in the straw alongside the astonished occupants - a mother goat and her new-born twins.

"Aunt Mary always kept goats . . ."

"They shared their warm bedding with me, and even their milk supply," he remembered with a sudden smile. "The nanny goat was very understanding."

In spite of the pain in his ankle, Jean-Marie had snuggled up beside the goats and fallen into a deep and careless sleep.

"I was woken by someone coming to let the goats out," he said. "There was no point in trying to escape - my captors were only children. A little lad, David. And his big sister."

At first, seeing it as their Great Secret the children had brought him food smuggled out from the kitchen . . .

"Like an Enid Blyton Adventure - 'The Famous Five to the Rescue.' "

"There were five of them," Jean-Marie said. "Five kids, bless them."

Before I came along, there would have been five of us, Rosemary thought. Five Fryer children.

But of course the grown-ups had soon discovered what was going on.

"And just as well," he said. "I was in a bad way. Delirious probably. My ankle needed attention. And in any case, I was in friendly territory. As long as people believed me when I told my tale, believed that I was French, Free French, it was OK."

They'd sent for the police, the grown-ups. They had to, of course. And the police got him to hospital. And then after intense interrogation and because he was under age, the family had been allowed to look after him until he was able to walk again on his damaged ankle.

"It's a wonder you weren't locked up, surely."

"I would have been but for this wonderful woman. Aunt Mary they called her. She faced up to the police, the army, everyone.

"He's only a lad," he could remember her insisting. "A lad with a broken ankle. What mischief is he going to get into, I'd like to know."

"Although the authorities kept tabs on me, I was taken back to the cottage. Everyone was so kind - the family and the village too. I was with them for weeks," Jean-Marie told her, a dreamy look coming over him. "Practically the whole of that glorious summer."

Eventually when the plaster came off and the ankle felt strong enough, Jean-Marie had to leave his temporary haven to set off for London and the Free French.

"So I never did find my way to the undercover unit."

"What about your brother ?"

"We met up again in London. He was killed later in France, poor bugger."

"I'm sorry."

"So many fine men . . . But where was I ?"

"When your ankle was better . . ."

"Yes. I had a police escort to the train, but as it started up that steep incline, I looked down and saw all of them - the five children, their mother and her aunt - there they all were in the orchard waving goodbye."

"Like a scene from that film, you remember, 'The Railway Children' . . ."

"That's right - all waving their hankies."

"What a wonderful story. Did you ever look for your rescuers ? Afterwards, after the war ?"

"No, I never did." And he sat there quietly remembering.

"I've dug out a couple of photos from back then. From the war," he said. "Thought they might interest you."

He cleared a space and spread them out on the table, a handful of faded and dog-eared black-and-white snaps. And Rosemary let out a gasp . . .

"Hey - what is it, ma chère ? What ever is it ?"

They were pictures of Billy, her lost boy, Billy. The likeness was uncanny.

"I'm sorry," she said. "For a moment . . . just for a moment . . ." But she couldn't go on. It was too painful.

He put a hand gently on her shoulder. "I think we need some fresh coffee," he said.

As it was the photos which had caused the pain, he began to gather them up to make room for the tray.

"No !" she cried. "Don't put them away. I'd like to look at

them properly. It was just that without my glasses, they reminded me of someone, a friend, who has recently died. I'm sorry - it took me by surprise."

With her glasses on, the likeness was stronger than ever.

She remembered that family gathering in Henry's garden for Julia's wedding. Seven, eight years ago. Julia and Marcus had three children now - Jeremy, Belinda and Sam. Jeremy away at Prep School. How the years had flown . . .

What was it Davy had said ? How had he put it ?

"Your Billy, he's a right enigma, Rosie. Must be a throwback, I guess."

"Oh shut up !" she remembered saying, half teasing him, half serious. "Our Billy's as much family as I am so don't you go stirring it up for me with your idiotic speculations."

And as they were leaving, Davy and Stella and their lot, hadn't he called out of the car window to her : "Rosie ! What we were saying. Billy. He does remind me of someone. Someone from way back. It'll come to me shortly. I'll tell you when it does. I can almost remember already."

But they'd somehow never got round to the subject again, not until the Memorial Service for poor Billy.

"You never told me who he reminded you of, Davy," she'd said.

"I wasn't sure myself," he'd told her gently. "There was someone in Somerset. Way back. Before you were born. Ask Aunt Mary about him. Maggie says I'm dreaming, making it up, but even though I was only four or five, I'm pretty sure there was a soldier or someone hiding in the goat house. Aunt Mary will know."

"Jean-Marie !" Rosemary said, "can you remember the name of the people who rescued you that time ? The name of the village ?"

"How could I ever forget," he said. "The village was called Isle St Agnes."

Rosemary put her hands up to her mouth in amazement. "Why didn't you tell me before ?"

"You didn't ask me."

"And the family ? Tell me about the family."

"The cottage belonged to a spinster lady, Miss Mary Petherton . . ."

"It was *my* family ! Don't you see, it was my family that rescued you."

131

"Mais non !" Jean-Marie was stunned at this. "But that's impossible."

"Tell me about them, please tell me about them."

"But you must remember it for yourself. You must have been David's big sister. Yes ?"

"No, no. I'm his younger sister. He's older than me. He was six, seven when I was born."

"I can't believe it. It's the craziest coincidence."

"Am I interrupting . . . ?" Hugo was at the open door.

"No, no - we've just discovered the most amazing link between us. You'll never believe it."

"I'm sorry, but I've an urgent message for you Mr Honoret. Louisa has been trying to phone you all morning. It's your wife . . ."

"Oh, lord - what is it, man ? Is she . . . ?"

"She's gone. She's dead. Slipped away in her sleep. They've been trying to contact you."

"Poor soul," said Jean-Marie dashing out to the car. "My poor Elize."

After so much excitement, so many revelations, Rosemary could settle to nothing.

"I'm going into town," she called to Hugo. "Must phone home. Won't be long."

But she couldn't get through to Betsy.

What about Davy ? She rang the surgery. Sarah, his receptionist, said that Mr Fryer was out on his rounds.

"Tell him Rosie called. From France. Tell him I'll try again tonight."

But she didn't.

By evening Rosemary was being swept away by developments. By then things were moving too fast for her.

Having stocked up with necessities at Bon Marché and sorted them out at home, Rosemary felt quite exhausted. The sky was darkening as usual, and as the first clap of thunder sounded she gave up any pretence of useful activity, and scurried up to bed. Curled up with a hot water bottle clutched in her arms, she slept like a baby.

It was dark when she woke, not storm dark but evening dark. She pulled on warm comforting clothes - jeans and the soft baggy grey jersey. Tidying the bedclothes before she went down to make herself an omelette, she suddenly felt a need to handle her nine little friends again, to tell them that Jean-Marie had been in Isle St Agnes, that he'd known Aunt Mary and Mother and everyone. Yes, she must tell them.

Rosemary took the box down from the beam and was just spreading the mannikins out on the quilt around her when she heard a car draw up at the gate. She scrambled off the bed to see who was coming, but Jean-Marie was already across the yard and banging on the door.

"Rosemary, Rosemary !" he called, letting himself in. "Rosemary, where are you ?"

Leaving the little carved figures where they lay, she ran down and into his arms.

He lit the fire while she made supper. He opened a bottle of wine. She found some Mozart on the radio.

Rosemary glowed with happiness. She found there was the most astonishing intimacy in these small shared tasks.

"You'll think I'm utterly heartless," he said, "coming straight here from her death bed."

"I don't think anything," she said. "I'm just happy to have you here."

Shameless as it seemed in the circumstances, there were strong electric currents between them tonight which had nothing whatsoever to do with the storm that was flashing dangerously across the valley of the Charente.

"Do I have to leave . . ." he asked shyly.

"You can't drive all that way in this."

"I could go to Louisa's."

"There's no need for you to go at all."

"Do you mean it, chérie ?"

"I'd like you to stay."

"Are you sure ?" Jean-Marie asked. "I'm an old man."

"You're not - not to me."

"You're very sweet, but I'm - "

Rosemary put her finger on his lips. "It's how old you **feel** that counts."

He grabbed her to him in a bear hug. "With you, well . . ." And bursting into song, he danced her wildly round the table. "**You make me feel so young . . .**"

It was so cosy, so right, so comfortable, to be checking the fire, locking the door, preparing for bed. Together.

"You go up," she said, after he'd finished in the bathroom. "I'll only be a minute."

Until now, Jean-Marie had never been upstairs in the farmhouse.

He was amazed at the huge old bed, piled high with pillows and the plump duvet. And lo-and-behold he was able to scramble aboard without using the mounting block.

And then . . .

And then he saw the set of carved figures scattered on the quilt. Where she'd left them earlier.

Of course he recognised them instantly.

"Betsy, my Betsy !" he whispered, with astonishment and understanding. "My sweet Betsy !"

*   *   *

Chapter Twenty-Two

As the ferry pulled away from the dock, Rosemary went up on deck to wave to the fast-diminishing figure on the quay, Jean-Marie Honoret.

"It's crazy," she'd said, when he'd told her his plan. "If you come up to see me off, how the devil are you going to get home again, uh ?"

"I'll hitch a lift back here," he'd said confidently, "if Mr Forêt will let me leave my car in his yard."

"That's no problem," Hugo had said, and she realised with relief that the antagonism between the two of them had completely evaporated. Literally, overnight.

"If I don't get a lift, I'll come back on the train."

Now Rosemary watched the bright lights of Le Havre until they disappeared over the horizon and all was inky black.

He would follow her to England shortly, once the funeral was over. His wife's funeral. Just for a holiday.

"We'll go down to Somerset," she'd promised him. "The goat shed's still there - we'll see if you can still squeeze into it."

Yes, they would have a few days together in Aunt Mary's cottage. Catching up on one another's lives.

No wonder Aunt Mary had been so determined to make certain Rosemary found the wooden nine-pins. She must have been waiting for an opportunity to give me them, Rosemary realised, to tell me the story behind them. But Fate (in the form of a stroke) overtook her, left her speechless, prevented her from fulfilling the promise she had made to her sister Betsy so many years before.

"Don't tell her, Mary, not until I've gone. I wouldn't like her to think badly of me. Any of them to think of me as a slut, a scarlet woman."

"They won't think any such thing," Aunt Mary had protested, fully aware of the damage that Norman Fryer had done to all the girls, Rosemary included. "I think they'll be glad for you, Betsy, love. Glad to think that you had a taste of happiness."

"Oh, don't say that, Mary. He wasn't as bad as you like to make out. I was weak. Weak and silly. And after Rosemary came along, well . . ." **Who was I to accuse him, to accuse anyone ?** she'd wanted to say, but her voice failed her. She was still - then, so many years later - deeply ashamed of herself. Overwhelmed by guilt.

"That was the trouble," Aunt Mary had told her, no longer able to hold back her anger. "You were too bloody guilty to confront him, weren't you ? One after the other, that damned man abused the children . . ."

"Oh, don't. Don't. It couldn't have been as dreadful as you say. I can't believe it of him."

Not her Norman, surely. Not Norman Fryer, upright member of the community. Assistant manager at the bank, church warden, air raid warden, long-serving local councillor - no ! Surely not.

But in her heart Betsy Fryer knew very well that it was true. Horribly true. Never mind her own guilt. If he'd known (and she sometimes thought he did know that their youngest was not his child), that would simply have given him a convenient excuse to start his games on poor little Rosie. All along Father had been messing about with the girls, one after the other, and long long before there was anything for Betsy to feel guilty about. But she'd still never found the courage to denounce him, confront him.

"Your damned guilt," Mary exploded, "yours was nothing, *nothing* compared to his."

"I know you're right," Betsy had said. "There's not much I can do about it now. The damage has been done."

"There is, though. You can tell them, apologise, try to explain how it was with him."

"I can't, Mary. I'm not strong like you." If only she'd been stronger there might have been no skeletons in the Fryer family cupboard.

"Not even now the bloody man's gone ?"

"I simply can't," Betsy had sobbed. "But you can, Mary. One day. When I've gone too. Rosemary must be told."

Neither Aunt Mary nor poor Mother could ever have dreamt who would tell Rosemary. Nor in what circumstances.

Now in the Forêt family's marital bed with the thunder and

lightning crashing around the old farmhouse, the truth was finally coming out.

Glowing with tenderness and anticipation, Rosemary had run lightly up the rickety stairs to join Jean-Marie in bed.

"No," he'd said, holding her away from him. "No, my dear, it cannot be."

It's Elize, Rosemary had thought. It's all happening too fast, too soon. He's a man of integrity. In my eagerness, my selfish eagerness, I've ruined everything. And feeling deeply ashamed of herself, she perched awkwardly at the foot of the bed, pulling a soft brown blanket up round her shoulders.

But of course it wasn't Elize at all.

"Where did these come from, ma petite ?" he asked, having made her accept that there was only going to be talk between them tonight. "These funny little skittles - who gave them to you ?"

"My Aunt Mary," she said.

"And did she tell you anything about them, where they came from or anything, your Aunt Mary ?"

"No. She couldn't. By then, she couldn't speak at all." And sadly Rosemary told him all about it. About those last days in Orchard Cottage. "The funny thing was, if funny's the right word, that she was determined, absolutely determined that I should find the box and the skittles. It was literally her dying concern. You know, on her actual death-bed, with her dying breath. And yet everything was to come to me anyway, so why the panic ?"

"Just as well she did," he said. "We were in grave danger, you and me."

"Danger ?"

"Danger of committing an unforgivable sin . . ."

"Sin ?"

"Incest."

Incest ? What was he saying ? What did he mean ? There'd been more than enough incest in her life. Not more incest, surely.

"My dear girl, my first-born, my English daughter - don't you understand ?"

And at last she did.

"Come here, my child," he said holding his arms out to her. "I am surely allowed to cuddle my long-lost daughter."

137

"Heavens !" she said, disentangling herself from his embrace to snuggle quite shamelessly in beside him. "You're right. Aunt Mary stopped us. Saved us . . ."

From repeating the dreadful pattern of abuse in the Fryer family. And sometimes sobbing with the shame of it, the pain of it, she told him a little about Father and his dirty games.

"My God ! He must have been a beast. You poor darling. You and all your sisters. And my poor Betsy. He should have been locked up. Castrated. The beast !"

It had affected all their lives, she told him. Maggie, Frances. Poor old Kate . . .

"She's never recovered from it, poor old Kate." She'd had a successful teaching career, ending up Head of a village school up in Yorkshire, with a School House and all. But always alone. Bitter and lonely. "She has nothing to do with any of us, Kate. Hasn't had for years. Didn't even come to Aunt Mary's funeral. That bloody man . . ."

"But at least he wasn't your father, my love."

No - he wasn't my father, Rosemary thought. With a great surge of relief. **He wasn't my father** !

"The little nine-pins saved us."

"And only just in time, er - Papa !"

They laughed aloud at that in sheer delight. Jean-Marie made them a nest of pillows and began to tell her the story of the skittles.

"I carved them for her, for your mother, all through that next winter, in between action. There was a lot of lying-up, lying-low, waiting for opportunities to strike. I spent all that waiting time making these small gifts for my beloved Betsy. I thought she could perhaps pass them off as toys for the children. That she'd find a way to keep them."

"Of course, what you didn't know was that while you were giving life to the nine-pins . . ."

"She was giving life to our love-child."

"Didn't you know, didn't you guess ?"

"It never occurred to me. I was young and innocent, don't forget. I was a virgin. When it started between us, I was a virgin."

"Why didn't you try to find her ? You know, after the war ?"

"She was a married woman, wasn't she. With an exceptionally unpleasant husband. Much as I loved her, I felt it was best to lock it away in my heart, the magic of that summer in Somerset. For her sake. Though if I'd known about the baby . . ."

"Yes ?"

"Who knows. I sent the nine-pins to Orchard Cottage one-by-one as I finished them, smuggling them over one way and another. The odds against me surviving to complete the set were not strong . . ."

"Thank goodness you did, my dear," she said, hugging him fiercely. "Thank goodness you survived."

"Aunt Mary knew where they were coming from, who was sending them. Your mother must have asked her to keep them for her, to keep them hidden, because of your father . . ."

"No, come on now, get it right, mon père - because of Norman Fryer, OK!" Davy's father, Maggie's father, everybody's father except Rosemary's. Praise the Lord !

"There was one thing - I don't know whether it reached her but after the war, throwing caution to the winds, I sent her a postcard."

" 'Remembering always.' "

"How did you know ?"

"I have it here - look." And she took it out from the bottom of the brick box. "Why do you think I went down to St Julien, eh ?"

"So if I hadn't sent it, we'd never have met."

"You've the card to thank, the skittles . . ."

"And your Aunt Mary."

The storm had died away by now. It would soon be light.

"Rosemary," he said, meditatively. "In France we have this tradition. We say that rosemary stands for . . ."

"For remembrance !" Rosemary cried. "It's the same in English: 'Rosemary, Rosemary - that's for remembrance'. It was her secret message for us. For us both. Don't you see ? I was her rosemary, the proof of her brief happiness, a flesh-and-blood reminder. Oh, Mother !"

"Oh - my dear Betsy !"

"I think we need a drink," they said together. And he went down for a bottle and glasses.

"We mustn't spill wine on the sheets. Hugo's sister does the laundry and she'd think the worst."

"She'd think we'd had an orgy."

"Which we nearly did !"

139

They laughed and knocked back the wine and set out the little men around them again. And Rosemary identified each of them for him :

"Father . . ."

"Please, *not* father."

"Sorry. Norman-Bloody-Fryer, Fred Sixsmith, Pete, Edward . . ."

"They weren't all bad lots."

"True. Here's my Billy, and Laurie-bless-him, Hugo Forêt . . ."

"No wonder the poor chap has been a bit aggressive with me. Thought I was stealing you away, didn't he."

"And number eight . . ."

"Yes ?"

"That's you, you old darling. My real Dad."

"But hang on, what about number nine ? Is there someone you're not telling me about ?"

"No, no. No-one else."

"Then it is a good omen, the ninth figure. It stands for the man who is still to come into your life, the man who will really bring you happiness."

"I can't imagine being happier than I am now," she said.

"Nevertheless, it promises you romance and love. The finding of your soul-mate. So don't argue."

"But how can they look so much like the men in my life, your nine-pins ?" Rosemary asked, sleepily.

"Heaven knows, my dear. The faces I carved were those of my companions, my Free French comrades. As near as I could manage."

"And yet . . ."

"Any likeness you must be imagining, right. You've found in them the faces you were looking for."

"No, no ! Surely you can see the strong differences between them ?"

"To be honest with you, I can't. To me they look like a more-or-less identical set of skittles."

"Well then . . . I must be going crazy." It had seemed so clear, the likenesses had seemed so strong - was it all in her head ? A trick of her subconscious ?

"It might have been magic," he said. "There's a lot of it about."

140

They dozed a bit, and as morning broke Jean-Marie carried on with his story.

"After they'd found me, your brother David . . ."

"**Davy**. He was always known as Davy."

"After Davy had found me in the goat shed, Davy and was it Kate ?" he told her, "your family took me in. It was against all the rules, of course. By rights I should have been incarcerated until the police had checked out my story. Your Aunt Mary was incredible - battling it out with first the police and then the army. What a character!"

"She certainly was a character."

"There were all those kids, bless them. And your mother and your Aunt. And it was the tiniest cottage - I don't honestly know how they made room for me."

Through all that hot dreamy summer, with British bombers flying in and out of Yeovil and regular enemy attacks on Taunton and Exeter, Jean-Marie had shared the simple life of the large noisy Fryer family, evacuated to their Aunt Mary to escape the Bristol Blitz. And Father.

And that's when this tall blond Frenchman, scarcely more than a lad, fell in love with Betsy Fryer, mother of five and twenty-something years his senior.

A bit like me and Edward, Rosemary thought with a shock. The Toy Boy thing. It must be genetic.

"That's what struck me, ma chère, that day in Bruno's bar, the first time I saw you - your likeness to my, my Betsy. Half a century later and it stopped my heart. Knocked me off my rocker. You look so much like her."

"She was a good deal younger than I am - then." Betsy Fryer had been thirty-nine when Rosemary was born.

"Most improper, most unfortunate," the elderly biddies in Isle St Agnes had sniffed. "Another one ! At her age !"

"Good job they didn't know the truth of it then," Jean-Marie laughed. "That would really have offended everyone."

"Apart from Aunt Mary."

"Mary Petherton was a gem. I wish to God this had all happened sooner, before she died. I have so much to thank her for." And with a sudden flash of understanding he remembered something that had mystified him at the time.

"When's your birthday, Rosemary ? You didn't tell me."

"March," she said. "March the twenty-first."

"The spring equinox . . ."

"That's right. I've always felt it was a bit special. The equinox *and* the very start of the Zodiac year. The first day of Aries . . ."

But Jean-Marie wasn't listening. He'd climbed down from the bed to lean out of the window.

"That means," he began. "What that means is . . ." and Rosemary saw his eyes were brimming with tears.

"Hey, hey - come on, now."

"No," he said. "Believe me, these are tears of joy."

She got out of bed and joined him at the open window. He put an arm round her and held her close.

"On Midsummer's Eve, we went off on bikes, Betsy and I. Once the children were in bed, right."

"You cycled ? How about the ankle ?"

"It was out of plaster by then and not giving me too much trouble. In any case the prospect of this outing together, alone together, Betsy and I, was more than enough to heal me."

"I don't know . . . !"

"It was your Aunt Mary suggested it. We took a picnic and a bottle of wine that she'd been keeping for a special occasion. We cycled to Glastonbury and climbed the Tor and celebrated the midsummer sun rise and . . ."

"And that must have been where I came from !" The date was right, certainly - June 21st : March 21st. Wow ! Imagine being conceived at dawn on midsummer's morning. A love-child. On Glastonbury Tor. Pure magic !

"It was still light when we set out which was fortunate because of the blackout. And I remember . . ."

"Yes ?"

"I remember so clearly that from our grassy nest on top of the Tor we could see the sky lit up in all directions."

"What was it ?"

"It was the blitz - the sky was red, red with the fires of Exeter, Bristol and maybe even Cardiff."

"But surely they were too far away. Miles away."

"It wasn't the burning buildings we saw but the reflection of the flames on the clouds. We'd found our bit of heaven there in the

142

midst of those hell fires. I'll never forget that night. And then the sunrise . . ." His voice trailed away. "I don't suppose I should be telling you all this, ma fille, but . . ."

"But I am a grown woman. A woman of the world."

"I'm a bit slow in the uptake. I'm only just realising the significance of what happened soon afterwards. How Aunt Mary suddenly insisted on sending Betsy home to Bristol, to Norman one weekend, only a couple of weeks later. I remember I was sick with disgust at what he would be doing to her, and I had so little time left in England. My ankle was practically better. I was simply waiting for instructions from my unit and my adventure in Somerset would be over. I took it very badly. I didn't understand . . ."

"How could you ?"

" . . . that Aunt Mary was sending your Mother back to her husband in order to protect her, to 'legitimise' the pregnancy."

"That must be why she was always so fond of Billy, Aunt Mary," Rosemary realised. "Billy was so like you, love." So like his unknown grandfather. "I wish you could have known each other, you and Billy." It might have made a difference.

Rosemary went down to make a pot of tea. Back in bed she had a sudden thought.

"Jean-**Marie** - Rose**mary**," she said. "I wonder if there was more to it - I wonder, could Mother have chosen my name to, as it were, echo yours . . ."

"As an echo of mine ?!"

"Yes . . ."

"Yes . . ."

And another piece of the jigsaw fell into place.

Apart from finding Jean-Marie, Rosemary thought as the ferry ploughed its way homeward, the best of it is that I am not after all the daughter of that bloody monster, Norman Fryer. In my case, it wasn't incest. He was a filthy old man, yes. But at least he wasn't my father. That makes it easier to bear.

Poor Maggie. Poor Frances. Poor old Kate - Rosemary could understood her a little better now. Living alone, bitter and alone. A successful teacher, apparently, though she must have retired by now. But a sad pinched soul. There was no mitigating factor for any of her sisters. Nothing to ease their shame.

143

But for Rosemary, memories of those years of sexual abuse were now a little less traumatising.

Shivering with excitement at the blessings that her summer among the sunflowers had bestowed on her, as well as the early morning chill, and seeing that she was now quite alone on deck, Rosemary leaned over the railings of the *William Duke of Normandy* and yelled out so that the whole world could hear her :

"Norman Bloody Fryer was not my father !"

The screaming seagulls seemed to echo her cry - not my father, not my father - until the words were swallowed in the ship's churning wake.

"Here I am !" Rosemary Richardson cried, standing tall and proud with her arms stretched up to the stars. "Here I am - my mother's secret joy ! The child of Jean-Marie Honoret - his much loved daughter !"

And gathering up her things, she scuttled in to the bar to treat herself to a double whisky.

* * *

Lightning Source UK Ltd.
Milton Keynes UK
UKOW052151171011

180477UK00001B/10/A